In Harlem's Way

A novel by Robert Pucci

IN HARLEM'S WAY

ISBN-13: 978-1482690323

ISBN-10: 1482690322

to all I have loved, and who have loved me

to Marina, without you this book would not be

Preface

I can only tell this story as I remember it. And as it's been over forty years since that day in June, a moment to address my memory, or lack thereof, is both fair and warranted. Truth be told, most events of my childhood have indeed vanished. As vibrant and palpable as they once were, as forcefully as I attempted to sear them into my mind, they are gone, as foreign to me now as if lived by someone else. Today, memories of my youth are like photographs, captured moments in time, put together in no particular order, existing haphazardly in a sealed container which must be pried open to be revealed.

I can see myself sitting on the curb in front of our Bronx home, staring down at the broken laces of my PF Flyers - shirtless in Yankee Stadium with a Joe Pepitone bat raised triumphantly over my flushed, sunburned face - falling asleep on the D Train with my father's hand wrapped securely around mine. No narrative, no connective tissue, just moments. I've yet to decide if time's slow and deliberate theft of our personal history is one of life's curses or blessings. I see merit in both.

But leaving that discussion for another day, and this confession aside, I can swear to you the events of which I will now speak are as clear to me as if they happened yesterday. Don't ask me to explain it; I have no idea how the brain works in such matters. Perhaps it's simply because it was a marking day. There was the me before and the me after. I just know I remember it. More than remember. I can smell, taste, hear, and feel it as if it were all happening right here, right now. I close my eyes and the memories return, thick and full, pressing around me with urgent vitality, and when I embrace them, pulling them close like a familiar blanket, I'm there once more.

It was June 1st, 1969, the day I first met a black man. I had seen many before that, but he was the first one I ever knew. His name was Jack Hutchins, and I was seven years old.

Chapter One

At a few minutes past three on the last day of school, which happened to fall on the final day of May in 1969, I was sitting quietly in the backseat of my mother's tan Cutlass Supreme. Which was no pleasant undertaking. And not because it was a bad car, or an old car. It was neither. It was reasonably new, with a good after-market paint job and a serviceable radio. In fact, one might go so far as to say it was a stylish car because of its history. My father, who was a New York City police officer, bought the car from the Department's motor pool, which was the home of wayward cars. Impounded vehicles which no one claimed for lack of funds, or fear of being arrested, were sold to the public at a discount, and my father picked up the Cutlass, which he promptly told us was used in a notorious bank robbery. He even showed us the small, round hole in the rear quarter-panel which he claimed was created by a twenty-two caliber bullet fired, without question, by police, during a high speed getaway, or rather, attempted getaway, as we now owned the car.

My brother Frank and I chose to believe this tale of high speed pursuit even though each time my father told it he would glance at my mother, who would blush and turn away with the hint of a smile creasing her lips. But some lies are so tasty, so intoxicating, so harmless to the general good of the world, you are obliged to believe them in spite of your good sense. And in such cases a lie is not so much a lie, but a fib. And what's a fib but an embellishment that has lost its way from the truth? And what type of person takes issue with the lyrical ease and poetry of a lost embellishment? Not me, and certainly not my brother, Frank. And that's how we rationalized repeating the story to everyone we knew as often as possible while adding our own imaginative musings to the legend of our outlaw vehicle.

In any event, what made sitting in the back of my mother's nice, reasonably new, former getaway car unpleasant was the smell. In a moment of haste, or possibly a lack of concentration if you believe my father, I had broken two bottles of milk while retrieving groceries from the backseat. Yes, milk was once sold in glass bottles. And a little-known fact concerning spilt milk, at least little-known to me, and most certainly the person who coined the phrase, "Don't cry over spilt milk," is that it cannot be cleaned. My father, who seemed aware of this fact, had me scrub, scour, launder, bathe, bleach, mop, vacuum, and shampoo the carpet for no less than eight days, but nothing, and I mean nothing, erases the odor of spilt milk. And though it had been a year since I had broken those bottles, and the carpet was long gone, torn from its roots by my father in a fit of olfactory rage, the smell of sour milk rose from the floor boards with pungent force, bringing to mind images of cheese and vomit.

But I was not sitting quietly in the backseat because of the smell, or the sweat beading on my forehead from the dense heat offered by the approaching summer, or even from the release of energy one feels after finishing another year of school, especially one as challenging as the second grade. I was quiet for I was always quiet. An observer rather than a participant. The kind of boy who feels things others don't seem to notice. Even adults. Especially adults.

My mother told me I was not always so introspective, so willing to stand in the darkness on the outside of the circle, away from the fire. She claims as a toddler I laughed easily and found great joy interacting with anyone and everyone in my path. She says I was even generous with my hugs and never the first to let go of a tightly held embrace. But her description of me brings nothing to mind. No images flash before my eyes, no warm sensations embrace my body, no long forgotten emotions clog my throat. I have little doubt that she is telling the truth, but I do not know the boy of whom she speaks.

The quiet boy. The boy who listened from a distance as others spoke. The boy who stood free of the masses yet felt every miniscule change in the energy which fills the space between people. That's who I recall. That's the boy I know. That's where my memory begins.

My brother Frank was altogether different. Eighteen months my senior, and a recent graduate of Sister Claudette's third grade class, Frank was the brand of boy who sees how much he can get away with then goes a little bit farther. Actually, a considerable distance beyond a little bit farther, but once you go beyond what you can get away with does it really matter how far?

I recall earlier in the year I was under the spell of the Roman Catholic Bible. For some unknown reason I came to believe it necessary to kiss the Bible each and every time I passed it. This was not asked of me by our parish priest. It was not taught to me by the nuns of Sacred Heart Private School. Nor was it given to me as a directive during a midnight visitation from an angel or saint. I have no idea why I was kissing Bibles save the knowledge that if I walked past one without pressing my lips to the parchment I would burn in everlasting Hell as sure as the sun rises and the moon pulls tides.

Under normal circumstances this was only a minor inconvenience, a situation that occurred once a week, on Sunday, when my mother would require Frank and me to dust off our dress clothes and accompany her to The Holy Rosary Church, Bible in hand. But when my brother uncovered my sudden pious peculiarity, he spent the next five days placing my grandmother's leather-bound Bible in locations that required me to stop and kiss it. It popped up on the toilet, the kitchen table, wedged beneath a cushion of our living room couch, and inside the basket attached to the handle-bars of my banana-seat Schwinn. I was averaging nineteen kisses per hour every hour I was awake, which even at seven years of age was a solid thirteen hours a day. And this is not counting the numerous occasions I would mysteriously wake from slumber to discover the Bible perched on the nightstand with my brother snickering across the room as the covers lifted and fell over his convulsing body. By the time my mother learned of my obsession, and my brother's merciless torment, my lips were so badly frayed that a twelve ounce jar of Vaseline was called into service to repair them. Such is Frank.

As I sat quietly in the backseat of the Cutlass, attempting to block out the stench of sour milk, I became acutely aware that the sounds of the city, New York City, the Bronx, were being drowned by the ever-changing music pumping from the radio. More specifically, music mixed with the snap, crackle, and pop of Frank's fingers banging frenetically at the controls. You see, my brother was continually in pursuit of the perfect song. What made a particular song perfect for a given moment was apparently beyond my limited understanding of the relationship between music and action. However, Frank was an authority, or so he told me, and I had no reason to doubt him as he routinely exhibited great taste in popular music. But that did not make his quest to hunt down the elusive, yet perfect song, any less annoying.

"Frank, would you stop with the radio, please?" My mother sighed, "My nerves are at the breaking point."

I assume she said this in the hope that Frank would stop whatever he was doing rather than have to take responsibility for her broken nerves and whatever long-term ailment such a break might set in motion. She was mistaken. Rather than surrender and admit defeat, Frank's ingenious way around this current dilemma, in fact his way around every dilemma, was to continue whatever questionable activity he was undertaking and skillfully misdirect attention elsewhere. Usually upon me.

"Hey Mick. Your epidermis is showing."

I had no idea what my epidermis might be, where I could find it, or how long it had been exposed to the world. But filling with shame over the knowledge it was available for everyone to see, and for who knows how long, I immediately set in motion to find it.

Like most boys my age, I first checked my zipper, assuming epidermis was a four-syllable word for penis one learned in the third grade. It was not. Mine was safely locked behind the steel and copper zipper found in my trousers. I next checked my nostrils. Thinking perhaps epidermis is Latin for snot. But I was clean and dry. I ran down any and all possibilities only to discover epidermis was not slang for ear-wax, finger-nail-dirt, corner-mouth-crust or eye-goop. I was out of ideas, but not out of shame.

"I'm starin' right at it for crissakes," Frank offered with exasperation as if the sight of my epidermis made him sick to his stomach.

My body began to tremble. I was prone to that during times of stress. Anxiety, trembling, and stuttering all went together hand-in-glove. And to a seven-year-old boy there are few things more stressful than not knowing what everyone else seems to know about you.

"Leave your brother alone," My mother protested in a weak, yet appreciated, attempt to come to my aide.

"But it's hangin' out for everyone to see," Frank countered, as if he were doing a good deed. "Supposing Mrs. Muscatello's out in front of her house sweeping the sidewalk when we pull up? She's likely to puke."

"Ma!"

I felt the word push past my lips before I planned to say it. It was the anxiety talking. The general rule between Frank and me, and it was a good rule, was no tattling, snitching, or seeking third party aid in times of warfare, which was generally of the Cold War variety. But I was under duress, needed an ally, and she was the only one present. The only one who could save me from Frank and my exposed epidermis.

"Frank, leave him alone or I swear to god . . ."

The trail-off sentence. That meant business and Frank knew it. I could see he was displeased I had broken our rules governing intra-fraternal combat, but he also realized he had taken this bit of persecution about as far as he could take it. So he ceased with his verbal assault and hit me with the coup de grace, the slow, deliberate laugh. This particular laugh mixes authentic amusement with the self-satisfaction of victory, or at least a down and dirty job well-executed. Generally speaking, when Frank would send this condescending laugh my way I'd want to bash his head in with a large stick. But sometimes, and this was one of them, I was happy to hear it because I knew relief was coming.

"Epidermis is skin."

Damn, I knew that. A few months prior Frank ran this same routine on Steve Levy who lived next door to us on Waring Avenue. In fact, he drove Steve to tears with it, which brought a visit from his mother to our mother. There may even have been a spanking involved. The stress of the moment mixed with the smell of sour milk must have kept my brain from remembering Steve Levy and his exposed epidermis.

I could see Frank was quite pleased with himself when he realized I remembered the Levy incident. He turned away dismissively, let go under his breath with one final laugh, and fired the kill shot into my bow.

"Numb nuts."

"Not another word, Frank," my mother barked.

We drove quietly. Well, quiet except for the ever-changing music and the staccato assault of tiny fingers on the controls. Frank's diversion worked like a charm as my mother completely forgot about the radio which switched rapidly from Tommy James and the Shondells, to The Beatles, to Sly and the Family Stone, and so on and so forth and scooby dooby doo.

"When does school start again?" She wondered.

"Not for two whole months." Frank grinned.

"God help me."

She glanced at him sideways, then mussed his hair to let him know she didn't really mean she wanted or needed divine intervention to survive having her boys home all summer, but instead would simply appreciate a little calm.

And then it happened. More than three notes of a single song played continuously. The perfect song, the only song that would allow this particular moment in time to reach the fullness of its gold medal potential, had been found. It was "Groovin'" by the Rascals and Frank sang along with the band.

"That would be ecstasy, you and me, LSD . . ."

LSD? My mother's head shot around like it was not connected to her neck. It's even possible it completed a full revolution, completely circumnavigating her torso, but it happened so fast I couldn't testify to it in court, except to say that I definitely heard her vertebrae crack.

"What did you say?!" My mother demanded.

"I didn't say anything," Frank responded.

"You were singing. What were you singing?"

"Oh, you mean the song?"

"Yes the song. What'd you say?"

10

And like an angel, Frank sang the proper lyrics.

". . . you and me, *end-less-ly* . . . groovin'."

He even put his hand gently on her forearm, the little turd. But despite the fact she was driving our car on a city street, my mother kept her eyes keenly on Frank. Probing his resolve. Checking for a weakness in his defenses. There were none. And Frank had plausible deniability on his side. As far as my mother knew, there was a chance, albeit remote, Frank was telling the god's honest truth. She studied him a moment longer, but ultimately decided to take his response at face value rather than go down the long, dark, dusty road of where he learned the phrase LSD. Which happened to be from the song, "Lucy In The Sky With Diamonds" by the Beatles.

She returned her eyes to the comings and goings along Eastchester Road and Frank took the opportunity to glance at me and wink. And that's why I could never stay mad at him for very long. Frank would tease and torment, play tricks, misguide, embarrass, and otherwise point out the elephant in the room, but it was never to be mean. Never out of cruelty. It was always for the purity of the laugh itself. He honestly believed, to the core of his being, that his skill as a prankster was so accomplished, and so clever, the recipient of his talents should appreciate and enjoy them as much as he did. To his thinking he never laughed at you, but with you, and if you weren't laughing it was your shortcoming. But, more than anything, he was one of those people, even shy of nine years old, who made you feel grateful when you were invited inside, allowed to be in on the joke, to stand beside him, and to share in that self-satisfied, aggravating laugh. I learned later in life that they call this rare but wondrous quality charisma.

Serenaded by Frank and the Rascals, we continued north on Eastchester Road when I noticed something peculiar. Our car was slowing. This caught my attention because we were between lights and there wasn't a great deal of traffic. We should be humming along nicely and I was at a loss to understand why my mother was pumping the brakes when I needed to get home and watch television. I sat up taller, directed my eyes toward the front windshield, and saw the reason. A six-man work crew was blocking the street from curb to curb. Beside them was a large, red sign that contained a hand-painted arrow and the word, DETOUR. My mom brought the Cutlass to a complete stop and took a long, deliberate look down the alternate route suggested by the arrow. I believe it was Williamsbridge Road and I could tell she did not like what she saw, or what she thought she saw. She reached her left hand out the opened driver's side window, executed a small side-to-side wave, and called to one of the men.

"Excuse me."

There was no response. Undeterred, she tried again. This time her voice was louder, her left hand waved more aggressively, and her right hand lowered "Groovin'" on the radio.

"Excuse me!"

One of the crew pointed toward the detour route and continued with his work, which was to watch one of the other men work. He must have been a supervisor. But whatever waited for us down that long and lonely detour route weighed heavily on my mother's mind because she honked, which brought a scowl from the aforementioned supervisor. The second honk brought him to the car.

"Is there any way we can get through here?" My mother opened her eyes wider than normal to give the illusion of helplessness.

"We're tearing up the pipes. You gotta go around to the Parkway and cut over," he offered as he chomped what appeared to be sixteen pieces of bubble gum.

"I just need to get across. I live just on the other side of the intersection on Waring."

I began to pay closer attention to this exchange because while it was true we lived on Waring Ave, it was not true it was just on the other side of the intersection. To my way of thinking this was not a fib but a lie, and a lie, while unwise to abide, is best paid attention to as it reveals intention, especially when offered by one's mother.

"It's too dangerous," he said, pointing at the torn up asphalt before us.

"So is going down Williamsbridge Road with two young boys in . . . ."

"Can't do it."

He cut her off. He did this because he knew what all New Yorkers know. If a person is not getting what they want and you let them finish a sentence, there will be another sentence, and another, and another. The discussion will never end. But if you cut them off, the issue is closed. There might be facial contortions to deal with, perhaps a hand gesture or two, but the oral argument phase of the debate is terminated because you've let them know you're aware of every possible counter-argument they may raise and you've dismissed the lot of them. Best they surrender in silence and save their sentences for another day.

My mom gave him the evil-eye for the requisite three seconds then said, "Thank you," with deliberate and

perfect enunciation, lingering on each syllable and providing a slow, yet heavy, emphasis on the "kuh" sound of
"thank." That was her way of saying "F-you" while her
children were present. Frank knew it, I knew it, and my
mom knew we knew it, but, like many things in life, the
appearance of decorum is often more important than
decorum itself. So the supervisor got a long, drawn out,
almost sincere sounding, "Thank you." And he knew it.

My mom rolled up her window, turned toward the
backseat, and said in a soft, yet firm voice, "Michael,
close your windows. Frank, you too. And lock the door."

My brother and I looked at her in utter disbelief.
Locked doors were one thing, but it was a boiling ninety-
three degrees in the shade and she wanted us to close the
windows in a car without air conditioning and still har-
boring the smell of age-old milk?

"Can't we leave them half . . ."

"Close them!"

She'd cut off Frank. With exclamation no less.
This was serious.

Despite the barrage of honking horns coming
from our rear, my mom waited for us to seal the car tight
before following the detour sign east onto Williamsbridge
Road. I found myself growing concerned about what had
her concerned. I hadn't witnessed this level of attention
paid to automobile security since my father took us to a
drive-through safari park somewhere in west Jersey.

But it didn't take long for our surroundings to
change. The first thing I noticed through the glass of my
window were the cars. They were older models than I was
accustomed to seeing around town. They were also more
damaged, with large patches of gritty rust taking hold

where metal had been scraped or torn open. In fact, few of the vehicles I saw had a cohesive paint job. Nearly all were a combination of the car's original color, a primer, a new color, a second new color and rust. And I'm not even mentioning the holes, which seemed too large to have come from a .22 caliber bullet.

Then the buildings pulled my focus. They weren't necessarily older than buildings elsewhere in the city, they just had the appearance of it. The paint had long faded and was peeling in large quantities from the outer walls. Roofing material, what there was of it, was ravaged by the sun and maintenance of it had been long forgotten. Gutters, held to the fascia by bailing wire, were hung at odd angles and filled with so many holes, I have no doubt the rain water poured in every direction save the direction it was intended to flow. And then there were the windows, or lack thereof. There were openings to be sure, but few windows. In one building, I counted eighteen windows, six of which were filled in with cardboard, two with aluminum foil, and three with old, soiled blankets.

We continued deeper into Williamsbridge Road territory when it suddenly dawned on me it was unnaturally, and eerily, quiet in our car. Frank had completely turned off the radio as if to avoid detection, like a submarine running silent and deep in enemy waters. It was at precisely that moment I realized what had my mother concerned. Why she hit the supervisor with that "Thank You." Why she insisted we lock the doors and close the windows in a smelly, sweltering car like we did that afternoon my father drove us through a park filled with lions and tigers and bears. Why my brother sat motionless in the front seat, biting his lower lip, allowing silence to occupy the place normally filled by the perfect song. The neighborhood we were driving through was not just poor. It was black.

My eyes targeted the owner of a shoe repair store as he carried large, overflowing bags of trash to an already full can near the curb. He was old, but not quite as old as my grandpa, though both of them had snow-white beards and curved spines. I watched in particular the way his clothes moved on the air as he walked. Like they had a mind of their own. Pulling from his body as if they were made for some larger man and wanted to return to their original owner.

I watched three young girls playing jump rope. Not with rope, but with wire, thick, frayed telephone wire so heavy that swinging it high in the air strained their arms. I watched their muscles shake and struggle to keep the arc true and in motion, but eventually give out, bringing the game to a premature end.

Then there were the boys, a variety of ages, climbing a fence that led to an abandoned lot where others had erected a basketball court. The backboard, made of cheap, splintered plywood, was nailed to the brick wall of the adjacent apartment building. A toilet seat, bore out to fit the diameter of the dirt-coated ball, was called into duty as a hoop. And bicycle chain was used in place of netting. It seemed to work rather well until the ball was dribbled on a hidden, but apparently sharp, object which released all the air from the game.

It was people. Doing chores. Killing time. Flirting. Arguing. Buying. Selling. Eating. Drinking. Snoozing. It all seemed normal. They seemed normal. But they were different, they were black; and that meant danger. That's what we knew. That's what we learned.

We continued at a steady pace, my mother's eyes rising toward the looming traffic lights as we approached each and every intersection, imploring them to stay, or turn, green. And between lights the three of us looked at the people outside the car and realized the shop owners, the mothers with their children, the young men huddled at the entrance of the candy store, the elderly no longer at work, and the commuters in their cars were looking back. Watching us. Watching this white family drive through their neighborhood. I suddenly felt like the small guppies we kept in the fish tank my father brought home the Christmas before last. The guppies which all had died within a month.

Suddenly my body jerked forward and tires squealed as my mother slammed on the brakes. Distracted by the comings and goings outside the confines and safety of our car, she nearly drove us through the red light of a busy intersection. Fortunately, she was able to skid to a loud, ear-splitting stop before barreling into the pedestrian walkway like a battering ram. In so doing, she avoided colliding with a fruit peddler who paused long enough to give us an earful of driving instruction combined with a good look at the middle finger of his left hand.

We watched him grumble and push his weather-worn cart toward the sidewalk when a loud THWACK echoed from the rear window. The three of us jumped and turned our eyes toward the back of the car where an old man, dressed in rags, tapped on the glass with swollen knuckles.

"Change?"

He was tall and lanky and his skin was ashen and spotted with white dust. Sores covered his cheeks and he was most certainly without teeth, as his lips flapped when he spoke. He circled slowly around our idling car and approached the driver's side window. My mother sat still as could be, hands clenched on the steering wheel as if the old man's vision was motion-sensitive and by not moving she would become invisible and he would move on to another car.

He again tapped the glass and held out his hand which I noticed sported an old, silver wedding band which was now too small for his swollen finger.

"Change?"

My mother shook her head ever so slightly and stared at the traffic light, which to her dismay would not turn green. The old man looked into the car with tired, bloodshot eyes, and one last time begged through dehydrated lips.

"Just a coin, Missus? I'm powerful hungry."

The light mercifully turned, and my mother sped forward producing a faint wail from our churning tires. I looked back through the rear window and saw the old man catch a quarter tossed from the green, yellow and rust covered Plymouth behind us. He slipped the money into this pants' pocket, did a quick shuffle step of appreciation, and tipped his cap.

"Tommy Gorman's father said in Africa the big ones eat the little ones."

My mom looked at Frank who stared out his window with a combination of fear and curiosity.

"Tommy Gorman's father's an idiot."

Frank turned to face her as he formulated his response. He was proud and didn't like his information being dismissed so presumptively.

"Then how come we got the windows closed and the doors locked?"

"Don't start with me, Frank," my mother said, with anxiety raising the pitch of her voice.

Frank smiled the smile of the mischievous.

"Hey Mick, stick your arm out. Open the window, stick your arm out, and see if one of 'em eats it."

"Frank, I'm warning you," her voice rising.

But her warning fell on deaf ears. Frank reached over the front seat, took hold of the crank next to me, and began opening my window.

"Here, I'll help ya."

My mother's hand shot out and smacked him on the rear.

"I'm not foolin' with you, Francis! Mickey, close the window."

I'm sure the use of his birth name and the slap to his butt stung, even though my mother had no athletic ability and routinely hurt herself when trying to scold us. But Frank was enjoying the moment too much to care. It was a small price to pay for inflicting a touch of mayhem while establishing, at least to his mind, the validity of his information regarding activities inside Africa.

I closed the window as instructed and we finally reached the familiarity of Pelham Parkway, where another detour sign pointed north. Toward safety. My mother sped up, turned off Williamsbridge Road, and let out a sigh of relief as Frank turned the radio back on and sang his own version of "Groovin'."

"Moooovin', couldn't get away too soon. Nah, nah, nah, nah. . . ."

Frank laughed. My mother drove. And I sat quietly in the backseat, looking back toward the neighborhood that nearly claimed us. In time it disappeared, returning to whatever part of New York it came from.

"You can open the windows now."

My mother's voice was steady now and each of us opened our windows, letting in the fresh air which carried out the stench of sour milk and the heavy fumes of deep-rooted fear.

Chapter Two

It was now mid-afternoon, and my mother leaned against the formica counter of our undersized kitchen as she skillfully breaded chicken cutlets. With the dexterity of a surgeon, she dipped a pounded breast into a mixture of egg and cream, transferred it, without drippage, to a platter of seasoned bread-crumbs, then set it aside on Saran wrap for cooking later in the evening.

I enjoyed watching my mother cook. I found the steadiness and repetition of her movements soothing and it seemed to put my mind at ease when I needed it most. But today, as I sat at the nearby table sipping Ovaltine from my brand new Batman cup, I wondered what exactly these cutlets meant. They were my favorite, and as such, routinely made an appearance when a display of tenderness was needed to soften a painful blow. We had chicken cutlets the night we were told our puppy had been hit by a drunk driver. Chicken cutlets were served the night my father informed us that he had to cancel a trip to the Catskills we'd been looking forward to for three months. The list was endless.

"Katey's mom told me she's having a birthday party on Saturday," my mother said casually.

This topic was not cutlet-worthy, simply an unwanted nuisance. So hoping it was a rhetorical statement and not an invitation to a conversation, I simply took a sip of my chocolate milk and quietly licked the dark mustache it left on my upper lip.

"Mickey?"

It was not rhetorical. I stirred my drink, melting a smattering of granules that stubbornly refused to surrender their chocolaty goodness, and spoke quietly yet firmly.

"I don't want to go."

"Why not?"

"Cause."

"Cause why?"

"Just 'cause."

"Just 'cause why? And don't tell me 'cause you don't feel like it."

"But I don't."

"Mickey."

"What?"

"That's not what I mean."

"What did you mean?"

"I meant *why* don't you feel like it?"

There was no getting around this. I gave her 'cause, just 'cause, and what did you mean, but she wasn't having it. She wasn't giving up. She wanted me to go to Katey Finnegan's birthday party because she wanted me to be among my friends with whom she felt I no longer spent quality time. Or any time, for that matter. And since she was right, I had to answer.

"Cause she keeps tellin' everybody we're gettin' married."

My mother smiled, which I knew she would do, clearly not grasping the seriousness of such a claim in the world of soon-to-be third graders.

"Are you?"

"I'm not ever getting married."

My mother's smile slipped from her face and her pace slowed as she breaded another cutlet.

"Why not?"

"Don't want to."

"Don't you want to have a family?"

"No," I said firmly.

She then paused and considered her next question but I already knew what it was going to be.

"Don't you want children?"

"No."

My mother stopped breading and turned to me.

"How come you don't want children, sweetheart?"

The slow and deliberate manner in which she said those last words told me she already knew the answer, but wanted me to say it. To talk about it. To express myself and share what was inside me. She wanted me to guide her to the source of my decision to live a life without children, without a wife, without a family, without friends. Without connections. A life alone. But I wasn't about to.

"Just don't."

She started to reply when the outside door to the kitchen flew open. Frank, with a shock of dirt coating his forehead, charged into the middle of our conversation on a pair of Green Hornet roller skates. Out of breath, and panting like a horse who'd just run the Belmont, he rolled across the room and skidded to a perfect stop in front of the refrigerator. In one brisk motion, he jerked open the door, retrieved a pitcher of Kool-Aid, and downed half its contents without breathing.

"Frank. What'd I tell you about drinking from the pitcher? And don't come in here wearing those skates."

My brother snuck a peek from behind the pitcher, swallowed a gulp more, then tilted it from his mouth and delivered the news.

"Jimmy Junior hit me in the head with a dirt bomb."

Still panting, Frank went back to the pitcher, hoisted it near vertical and polished off the remaining four ounces of the purple-colored beverage.

"I'm goin' back out."

He deposited the pitcher on the counter, turned, and rolled for the door with all dispatch.

"Frank!"

He hit a fast, tight spin and stopped with his back to the door.

"What?"

"Where you going?"

"Nowhere."

"Who you going with?"

"Nobody."

"Take your brother."

Frank glanced at me sitting at the table.

"His skates are broken."

"Doesn't matter, take him with you."

Frank realized the conversation with my mother was burning valuable and diminishing daylight, so he relented.

"Come on," he said, with not even the decency of false enthusiasm.

"Nah," I said as I blew chocolate bubbles through my curly-cue straw.

"See, he don't wanna go."

Frank yanked open the door and was nearly in the clear when he was hauled back by my mother's voice.

"Hold it."

"The sun's goin' down!" Frank pleaded.

"Mickey, go with your brother."

My mother wanted me to get a little fresh air, as she said time and again. I wanted to watch *Dark Shadows*, which was starting in six minutes, so I considered putting up a defense. But ultimately I decided going outside was better than returning to the subject of Katey Finnegan's birthday party and my desire to grow up childless. So I slid from my chair and shuffled toward the door.

"Hurry up," Frank barked. "You're slow as shi..." Frank caught my mother's disapproving eye just in time. ". . . nola. He's slow as shinola."

Frank grinned, spun around, opened the door, and rolled into the late afternoon sunshine like the Green Hornet himself. I followed him with my Ovaltine, but as I heard the door click behind me I also heard my mother.

"Be back by six, your Uncle Pat's coming for dinner."

That's why we're having chicken cutlets. Uncle Pat. I pushed back into the kitchen quicker than I left it.

"What's he want?"

"To talk to you and Frank."

Across the loud, uncomfortable silence that filled the room, my mother and I looked at one another like boxers before a fight. She turned away first, returning to the safety of the chicken and the bread crumbs. I knew she wouldn't reveal the topic to be discussed, so I asked the second question that was on my mind.

"Why's he always coming here?"

"Because he loves you. Now go on."

There was more to it. I could see it in her face. She needed Uncle Pat to tell us something she couldn't tell us by herself, but I'd have to wait to find out what.

"Go on," she insisted.

I closed the door behind me, but with a harder and louder slam than the first time I slipped out behind Frank.

The next few hours moved by with the pace of a glacier. But as time does, it kept moving so at quarter after six I stepped into the doorway of the room I shared with Frank. He was on his bed, carefully dripping red candle wax into a bottle cap with the single-mindedness of a nuclear scientist.

"Dinner's ready."

"He here?" My brother asked without looking up.

"Ain't seen him but heard his truck park outside."

Frank's focus grew more intense as the wax approached the grooved edges at the top of the cap. Our summer blankets were cream-colored with yellow stripes and red candle wax spilled across their loveliness would not be tolerated by management.

"You comin'?"

"I'll be down in five minutes."

"It's ready now."

"And . . . so . . . am . . . I."

Finished filling his bottle cap, Frank put down the candle, snatched a baseball from the nightstand, and fired it at me like it was shot from a cannon. But I knew it was coming. It was a thing we did often because it was my gift. Catching. Baseballs, softballs, kick balls, soccer balls, rocks, melons, anything round, anything spherical, even snow-globes. My father used to say I had hands like a spider web. Said he never saw anything like it. I just wondered why of all the gifts out there, all the skills one might be granted, juggling, drawing, tree climbing, whistling, catching round objects was mine. I snatched the ball with one hand, never taking my eyes off Frank.

"You're a creepy kid," Frank said as we heard my mother call from the kitchen.

"Frank! Mickey! Dinner's ready!"

Before I knew what happened, Frank flipped himself off the bed, shoved me into our bookshelf and ran towards the door.

"Last one downstairs is eatin' elephant snot on the chicken!"

I recovered quickly, ignored the half dozen books that toppled to the floor, and gave chase. I caught him by the top of the staircase and we battled our way down, fighting for each step, competing for every inch of ground rather than sit through an entire meal with elephant snot on our chicken, imaginary or not. We reached the ground floor where our momentum carried us into the living room. And that's when a large hand shot up from the recliner and stopped us in our tracks.

It was Uncle Pat.

He was a big man, bigger than my father, who was his older brother by two years. Not heavy, mind you, just bigger. Perhaps three inches taller with shoulders as wide as a dining room table. He had told us those shoulders, along with the substantial biceps and thick forearms protruding from his shirt sleeves, came as a result of working twenty-two years as a load man for a cross-country trucking company. I think he was just born big. But I'm fairly certain the texture of his hands came from the job. They were abrasive like sandpaper and the knuckles were large and misshapen from countless breaks healed without thought of proper mending. But that hand, coupled with the newscast playing on the television, meant one thing. Be quiet. And even Frank wasn't so brave as to breach Uncle Pat's unwritten rules of living-room protocol. So we turned our attention to the television.

The news in 1969 was dominated by two events. The first was Vietnam. The three of us watched quietly as the newsfeed showed young soldiers firing into dense jungle. We couldn't see who they were firing at, but whoever it was appeared to be firing back as the soldiers looked panicked with fear.

The screen then cut to a helicopter hovering low to the ground, spraying dirt and debris as medics bandaged blood-soaked men slung like scarecrows across canvas stretchers. It was a horrific sight, and the camera lingered upon the bullet-ridden bodies long enough to make me want to turn away.

The second event to get prime-time coverage was the civil rights movement. Often this bit of news featured peaceful rallies outside schools and government buildings, but not tonight. Tonight the television brought into our home a clash between demonstrators who called for "black power" and white riot police who chose to speak with riot batons instead of words. I'm not exactly sure where it took place but it was a city, a northern city, perhaps Chicago. Maybe Newark across the river. Wherever it took place it was clubs and tear gas versus rocks and bottles. We watched quietly as the two sides were locked in a savage scuffle, and I found myself thinking that the two wars didn't seem all that different.

"Tommy Gorman's father said in Africa the big ones eat the little ones."

Uncle Pat glanced at Frank, then turned back to the television as a police dog chewed a man's leg.

"Wouldn't surprise me a bit."

"Dinner's on the table," my mother called from the kitchen.

Uncle Pat lifted his thick, heavy frame from the recliner and shut off the television, returning peace to our living room.

"How's everybody doing? Takin' care of your Ma?"

"Yes, sir," Frank replied.

"Gotta always take care of your women. That's job number one."

"We are," Frank assured him.

"Good."

He then turned his gaze in my direction and his grey-green eyes studied me longer than I liked.

"How you feelin'?"

"I'm okay?"

"Yeah? You sure? No problems?"

I nodded. Uncle Pat studied me a moment more.

"Okay. Good. Let's eat."

He placed one rough hand on each of our necks and steered us toward the kitchen, where my mom was doling out the cutlets.

"I don't want them watching that stuff. It gives them nightmares."

"Not me," Frank stated proudly as we took our seats. "Just him."

"Does not," I countered.

I was lying. It did give me nightmares. Horrible nightmares. I wouldn't always remember the images when I woke, but I felt the emotions and I knew where they came from. The tightness in my chest, the difficulty breathing, it all hailed from the nightly news. But I didn't want them to know that. Not with Uncle Pat one seat away.

"Kids have to know what's what," my Uncle Pat advised as he poured milk into our glasses.

"They know plenty," my mother insisted, trying to catch Uncle Pat's eye.

"You don't talk to anybody." Frank spoke the words with the cadence of a memorized mantra.

"Damn right," Uncle Pat said. "You keep your mouth shut and don't get in a car with no one. Get in a car with someone you don't know, you're a dead man. They'll never find your body, not ever."

"For god's sakes, Pat."

"These are things they gotta know. It's not like it was when we were kids. You listenin', Mick?"

I nodded and sliced my cutlet into equal-sized quarters.

"Can't we talk about something else?" my mother insisted as she looked at Uncle Pat. "Something good?"

I felt my stomach tighten. Whatever it was Uncle Pat came to tell us, whatever my mom couldn't tell us alone, she was in a hurry to get out. She didn't want to wait for it to emerge gradually in the flow of conversation. She wanted it said here and now.

"Something good?" Uncle Pat repeated. "You mean like how some boys we know are gonna spend the summer ridin' horses, swimmin' in a pool, shootin' bows and arrows . . ."

"I ain't goin' to no camp!"

The words shot from my mouth with the speed and force of one of those arrows.

Uncle Pat looked at me with a stare meant to convey authority.

"Why not?"

"I want to stay here. With Ma."

"It's a day camp, sweetheart," my mother said. "It's just over the bridge in Jersey. You and Frank will be home every night for dinner."

"Forget that," Frank stated as fact. "I ain't goin'."

"I don't believe you guys," Uncle Pat said. "It'll be fun. You two never even seen a horse a cop wasn't riding."

Uncle Pat smiled at his own joke. But I wasn't laughing. I felt the muscles in my body tightening. Felt my throat burn and my face flush. I turned to my mother, ignoring whatever Uncle Pat had to say.

"Why're are you making us go away?"

"It's not like that, baby."

"Then why can't we stay here?"

And there was a pause. It may have been only a few seconds, but at the time it seemed like an eternity. In that pause my mother glanced down at her plate, peeked at Uncle Pat, and finally turned to Frank and me.

"Your Uncle Pat and I have been talking . . . and we think it's best if we moved out of the city and into the upstairs apartment at his home."

"No!" I shouted, nearly coming out of my chair. "I want to stay here."

My Uncle Pat saw my body trembling and tried to address me in a calm, even tone.

"I know it's sudden, but there's plenty . . ."

"I'm not going!"

I cut him off. This conversation was over. I wasn't leaving my home. My father's home. The only home I'd ever known. And I wasn't going to be sent away to camp. And I wasn't moving in with him. But the "cut off" only works if you hold power. And I held none.

"Your mother's working full-time now," Uncle Pat said. "You two can't stay here alone. It's that simple."

I began to gulp air. I was growing more anxious, and more frightened and the stress was taking over my body, forcing the muscles in my arms and legs to throb.

"This is our house," I said. "I'm staying in our house."

Uncle Pat was losing patience, but he tried to make us understand.

"This neighborhood has gone down the toilet. It's getting more dangerous by the second. And you can't afford this house anymore. So stop thinkin' about your-selves and think about your mother. You know how hard this has been for her? You know she picked up extra shifts to help pay for all this?"

"She picked up extra shifts 'cause my father's dead!" I screamed at the top of my lungs. "He's dead and you want her for yourself!"

"Mickey!" my mother cried out.

"She's not yours!" I yelled.

Uncle Pat grabbed my arm. "If I were you I'd keep my mouth shut."

"Pat!" my mother hollered.

But he continued with what he had to say.

"Come Saturday you two are goin' to camp. And next month you're moving to Jersey and that's final."

My mother reached across the table and pulled his hand from my arm, which was now trembling violently.

"Mickey . . . Oh god."

And then it happened, as it happened before. My body lost control of itself. A seizure the doctors called it. I tumbled from the chair and hit the floor with a loud crack as my head banged into the linoleum.

"Mickey!"

My mother leapt from her chair and circled the table. "Frank, call the doctor!"

My body shook and spasmed as my mind, aware of what was being said in the room, went to the place it goes in these times. The place I hate. The place I'm tied to and cannot escape. Where fear grabs hold of me, pulls me back and forces me to stay, tells me this is where you belong.

The last thing I heard was my brother dialing the phone. The last thing I felt was Uncle Pat's coarse hand sliding beneath my neck. But then I was gone. I was no longer in my mother's kitchen. No longer in the safety and security of my home.

I was there.

"There"—was a coffee shop on the corner of Castle Avenue and Gun Hill Road. It was a bright blue Sunday afternoon and my father and I were sitting at the counter eating our breakfasts like a couple of gentlemen. I had strawberry pancakes smothered in butter and maple syrup. He worked on a cheese and tomato omelet, washing it down with sips of coffee made sweet and light with sugar and cream. I chose gulps of Hershey's chocolate milk to accompany my food. Both of us read the paper.

The shop was filled to capacity. But despite the noise of the patrons I could hear music coming from a nearby booth. Each table came equipped with its own miniature jukebox and speaker setup and nearly all were in use. The table nearest the counter where we were sitting was occupied by a young couple. Teenagers. They shared a single order of french toast and listened to Elvis sing, "Are You Lonesome Tonight?" I remember that clearly as the slow rhythm of the melody fought with the frenetic pace of the bustling diner. It made me smile. I even hummed along as I chewed my food.

It was a great day. The kind of day one feels lucky to be alive. And not because Frank was home sick with the flu. It was a great day because the sun was out, the winter air was cold and crisp, Christmas was not far off, and I was sitting like a man with my dad, eating a hearty breakfast and looking over the sports section to see what the New York Giants were up to on the gridiron that glorious afternoon. It was a perfect moment. That I knew. What I didn't know was that it would be the last moment of the life I had lived to that point.

I'm not sure what I heard first, the screams or the breaking glass. Perhaps they happened simultaneously. In whichever order it occurred, I couldn't make sense of the sounds, but my father did. In a fast, fluid motion he withdrew the revolver from the shoulder holster under his jacket and spun on his stool. Now standing, he pointed the gun toward the front door as his left hand held up his gold police badge.

I remember him yelling, "POLICE!"

Staring back at him, in shock and disbelief, were two men. They were young, probably not much older than the couple listening to Elvis. But they had guns. They had masks. And they were black.

Not expecting to find an off-duty police officer sitting at the counter when they broke the front door and pushed into the diner, their guns had yet to fix on a target. Their firearms, while held with determination, were not pointed at anyone in particular, but my father's weapon was aimed directly at the big one's head.

I'm not certain if there is a measureable sonic difference between the silence that accompanies calm and the silence that accompanies fear. Perhaps there isn't. Perhaps it's our ears and our minds that create the disparity. Whatever the reason, the silence at that moment was ferocious and paralyzing. It coated me with its power and squeezed me with bone-crushing force. It made me small. It made me weak.

And then the silence was broken. There was a reverberation. A shattering. I was looking directly at my father when I heard it. I remember the pattern of his five o'clock shadow, the dampness around his mouth from the coffee he'd yet to wipe with a napkin, the bent corner of his shirt collar lifted by the edge of his corduroy jacket, the tightness of his neck muscles, and the piercing focus of his pale blue eyes. Eyes which, in response to the noise, had turned to face me, turned away from the two young men who stood gun in hand at the entrance of the cafe.

Then I felt it. First the impact of air sent pulsing against me as the pressure in the room was violated. Then human matter. Skin, bone and blood. All three splattering against my face, wetting my cheeks and lips with their salted touch. And I watched as seven bullets ripped into my father in a matter of seconds. Two struck his head, the other five tore into his chest. There was white smoke filling the room and it engulfed him in a milky haze as his insides pushed out through the holes in his body.

And last came the sound. Explosions. Deafening gunshots. Nine in all, I would find out later.

Perhaps when this happened it all happened at once. Sights and sounds existing in a single instant. But when I come back to visit this cafe, when the fear calls me like an old but jealous friend, it happens slowly, each moment given the opportunity to live in its own space and time. Providing me with the unwanted opportunity to see it unfold with sparkling detail.

"Daddy's here. It's okay. Daddy's here."

As the patrons of the cafe scrambled in absolute horror, I began to hear those words over and over. I recognized the voice, but it wasn't my father. He was crumpled on the ground. Not moving. Not breathing. And I saw his blood gather beneath my stool.

"Mickey, come on, Daddy's here."

The voice kept calling and I began to wonder if it was him after all. Maybe he was calling to me from some other place. A safe place. Away from this coffee shop. Away from the grip of death. Maybe he wanted me to join him. To be with him always. Safe in his embrace.

"Daddy's here."

As the screams around me continued, I closed my eyes and let myself go, in hopes I would see my father's smile when I opened them. My mouth slowly, imperceptibly formed the word which eased from my lips.

"Daddy."

Slowly, I felt my body, light as a feather, leave the diner and all the terror it contained.

■■■

I was back. Back in my mother's kitchen. I felt my fingernails digging into the palms of my now bleeding hand. I felt the thick saliva filling my throat. The sweat soaking through my clothes, causing them to stick to my skin. The throb in my skull where my head hit the floor.

"Daddy's here."

My Uncle Pat continued to whisper the words as he gently ran his hand over my arms. My eyes opened as my body grew still.

"Good boy. Good boy." He smiled reassuringly. "You're okay."

I could see my mother looking at me, her eyes completely red and filled with tears. She reached down and I felt her cool, wet hands touch my hot face.

"Oh, baby."

Uncle Pat lifted me in his arms.

"Let's get him upstairs."

With my mother holding my hand, Uncle Pat carried me from the kitchen. My eyes were burning and it was hard to see, but I remember Frank standing with his back against the refrigerator, not moving, watching, and I knew the fear had touched him too.

It was dark when I woke. I knew it wasn't late because Frank was not in the bed next to mine. Still, I didn't know how long I'd been lying there. It could take hours to get away from that coffee shop, and even then the escape was never complete.

I looked toward the photograph sitting on the cluttered nightstand. It was an image of my father, smiling wide with his arms wrapped tightly around his two sons. It was taken by my mother at my cousin Jane's first Holy Communion the summer before. My mom liked the photo because she said all her men were dressed pretty for once. She used to keep it in her room, on her nightstand beside her rosary, but after my father died she kept it on mine. I took hold of it and brought it close as I tried to recall the sound of his voice. No matter what shift my father worked, no matter how long that shift might last, he made certain he was the last one to poke his head into our room to say goodnight and the first to open the curtains each morning to let the sun shine across our beds. I cannot recall a single day or evening when his face was not the first and last I looked upon - when his voice was not the first and last I heard. It was a ritual of love, father to son, simple in design yet possessing great power, and I missed it dearly after he was gone.

His own father had left home when my dad was nine. He never saw or heard from the man again and possessed no knowledge as to where he'd gone or why he'd left. My grandfather simply went to work one day and never came home. I believe my father's determination to be the first and last person we saw each day was born from that. I believe he wanted us to have the feeling of safety and security he did not. The kind which can only come from certainty. And I believe he worked so diligently to meet this obligation he set for himself because he knew, deep down, nothing was certain. There was no safety. No security. Only the illusion of it. He knew that from his work as a police officer. And after he died, I knew it too. But even so, my mother wanted my father's face to still be the first and last I saw each day.

In front of the photo was a silver dollar. It was given to me by my father the last Thanksgiving he was alive. It was minted the year I was born and he said it would always bring me luck. Frank got one too, but he spent his on baseball cards and bubble gum. I kept mine with me at all times. And I held it tightly in my hands when I heard Frank's voice.

"You all right?"

He was standing in the doorway. I nodded. And he didn't say anything more. For all his deviousness, for all his delight in stirring the pot, he never commented on this. Never made fun. Not once. Not ever.

"They talkin' about me?"

"Yeah."

I took hold of the nightstand and pulled it from the wall. Behind it was a vent for our heating system that connected to vents all over the house, including the kitchen, where my mom was speaking to Uncle Pat.

"You can't talk to him like that, Pat. And you sure as hell can't grab him."

"I'm sorry. But he's gotta know he can't . . ."

"I'll teach him what he's gotta know. Not you."

There was a short silence, then my mom said what I wanted her to say.

"Maybe this is a bad idea. Maybe it's too much right now."

"Carol, I know this is hard, but there's no choice. You can't leave them home alone in the city all day and you can't afford to go without working."

My mother took a deep, tension-filled breath and her voice cracked a she spoke.

"It's getting worse. It's been seven months. They said they would pass and they're getting worse."

"It's been three weeks since the last one. They said they'd get further apart and they are. He just needs time."

"Time? What time? There is no time. Don't you know what's happening? Can't you see it? He's going away. He doesn't talk, he doesn't play, he doesn't do anything." She began to cry. "I'm losing him and I don't know what to do."

They were both quiet a moment. Then my Uncle Pat spoke.

"Maybe the move will do him good. New environment and all. Besides, there are . . ."

Frank pushed the nightstand against the wall. He'd heard enough. He climbed onto his bed and stared at the ceiling where he had drawn the Milky Way Galaxy with glow-in-the-dark markers. He then grabbed the baseball off the nightstand and tossed it up, seeing how close he could get it to the stars without hitting them.

"We're gonna run away."

"What?"

"Just for a little while. Just long enough for Ma to think we're gone."

"Why?"

"So she'll be scared."

"Why do you wanna scare Ma?"

"So when we come back, she'll be so happy nothin's happened to us she won't move to New Jersey if we don't want her to."

I rubbed my father's silver dollar with my thumb and forefinger.

"Where we gonna go?"

"I don't know. Doesn't matter so long as she don't know." Frank answered as he placed the ball back on the nightstand.

"Think it'll work?"

"Yeah." He shut off the light and we laid quietly in the darkness.

"How do you know?"

My brother took a long deep breath and let out the sigh of the increasingly annoyed.

"Cause I saw it on TV. Now go to sleep."

Chapter Three

At 7:15 am Saturday morning, a black and grey bus sat idling in front of our house. It was old and in disrepair, like its driver. Both of them coughed, and wheezed, and did not appear in peak overall condition. Through windows tinted to deflect sunlight, I could make out a small army of my contemporaries raising Cain in the back of the vehicle. City kids banished by their underpaid, overworked parents to the country for a taste of clean air and a glimpse of green trees.

As the morning heat began to rise from the pitted sidewalk, my mother stood between Frank and me digging into the far reaches of her pocket-book. She'd been quiet all morning and only now uttered her first full sentence of the day as she withdrew her hand and gave each of us a dollar bill.

"That's for lunch."

My mom was not one to purchase an institutional lunch. She was a lunch maker. A talker and a lunch maker. Meat sandwiches stuffed into brown paper bags accompanied by conversation. The fact she did neither on our first day told me she was as nervous as me.

I slid the money into my pocket and stepped toward the bus when she grabbed hold of me, pulled me close, and whispered in my ear.

"I love you."

I didn't say anything, and it killed her.

Knowing the permanent injury caused by such a slight, especially when levied by one's child, I wish I could say it was a mere oversight. A simple omission made by an anxious seven-year-old boy on his first day of summer camp. But it wasn't. I wanted to hurt her. I was angry. Angry she was sending us away. Angry we were moving to New Jersey to live with my Uncle Pat. Angry my father was murdered in a coffee shop.

My core condition, my instinctual make-up, was to heal. The ability to put myself in someone else's shoes and feel what they felt was strong in me. It guided me. Made me hesitant to bruise another physically, mentally or spiritually. Unless the person hurt me. Then that part of me went cold. And my mother had hurt me.

I felt the muscles in her arms relax as she let go of her embrace. She looked into my eyes, searching for a glimmer of understanding, if not forgiveness. She found neither. She then turned to Frank and hugged him tightly.

"I love you."

"Love you, too," he said.

"Lady, we're gonna be late here." The bus driver growled from his seat.

"Take care of your brother," my mother whispered in Frank's ear as she kissed him goodbye.

"I will."

She let go, and Frank and I climbed onto the bus and walked past the driver, who smelled of cigarettes and Ben Gay.

"You have fun now. I'll see you when you get back," my mother assured us.

The driver shut the door as my mother called one last goodbye.

"I'll be waiting right here."

"I'll be waiting right here." One of the kids sang out in a phony, high-pitched lilt, bringing laughter and an unwelcome gaze from the rest of the bus.

Frank and I kept walking down the center aisle as if no one had said a word. We knew these kids. Not by name. Not even by sight. But we knew what they were because we all came from the same piece of bark. City kids born of Irish, Italian, or Jewish descent. That's who lived in our part of the Bronx. That's who filled this bus. And if you showed weakness, you got eaten alive.

Frank stepped just beyond an open seat and turned to face me.

"You take the window."

Frank wanted the aisle for two reasons. He was claustrophobic and didn't like being pinned on the inside away from the action, and he didn't want any of these kids messing with me. Frank was good that way.

As I slid into the seat and pressed myself tight against the window, I peeked through the glass and saw my mother wiping tears from her face. She saw me looking and waved. I didn't wave back.

Meanwhile, Frank pulled up his pant leg, pushed down his socks, and retrieved a large, unopened bag of Bazooka Joe bubble gum he smuggled from our house.

"Who wants gum?"

By the deafening cheer which rattled the windows I knew my brother had just made twenty-three new best friends. I sat quiet and still, watching my mother continue to wave.

Camp Silver Birch was a poor man's camp. Not that I had ever seen a rich man's camp, or any camp for that matter, but this one had to be the bottom of the barrel. In fact, if you lifted the barrel and looked beneath it, you'd find Camp Silver Birch. The grass was made of dirt. The buildings looked like the concrete bunkers you see in old science fiction movies from the fifties. The ones frightened citizens hid inside to escape the radioactive waves of the H-bomb. The horses, which had the appearance of large goats, if not already dead, soon would be. And the leaf-filled pool reeked of chorine. Which I suppose, with a few hundred kids peeing in it, was a necessary evil. But it burned your nostrils to stand near it, let alone what it did to your eyes when you were in it.

When we piled off the bus, along with kids from a dozen other busses, the counselors separated us into groups of twenty. To this day, I have no idea what the criteria for putting a group together might have been, as it seemed as haphazard as throwing a handful of pennies down a well. But groups they formed and Frank made sure to keep me close at hand so we would not be separated. As it turned out, we were the Ojibwa.

"O-what?" Frank asked our young, eager, pimple-faced counselor.

"Ojibwa. They're a tribe of American Indian. One of the largest. Ranged all over the country."

Apparently whoever put this dump of a camp together thought it would be charming to incorporate an Indian theme for we, the underprivileged, second-generation immigrant youth of the great city of New York.

"If you'd rather, we can go by Chippewa. Another name used by the Ojibwa was Chippewa."

"Who gives a crap. Let's go to the pool," came a reply from one of the bigger kids in our group.

"I'm sorry, but there'll be no cursing here."

There were two types of counselor at Camp Silver Birch. One type was doing community service for undisclosed crimes against the state and didn't concern themselves with what you did or said so long as you were alive at the end of the day. The other was suburban do-gooders who wanted to help the unfortunate and instruct us in the etiquette of Connecticut. We had the latter.

"And the angel who hides in my pocket would appreciate it if everyone respected that rule."

Our counselor was quite taken with himself.

"Sorry," the big kid said.

"Apology accepted."

"Now can we go to the pool before it fills up with piss from all these homos?"

Inside the bunker operating as the boy's locker room, the Ojibwas were busy tearing off clothes and pulling on bathing suits, which mostly consisted of cut-off play pants. In the twenty or so minutes since we arrived at Camp Silver Birch, Frank had already begun drifting away from me. It was not his fault. Kids sought him out. Competed for his company. He couldn't remain in lock step with me if he wanted to. And I believed he wanted to as I saw him looking past his new friends to make sure I was okay. He had assured our mother he would take care of me, and Frank was not one to make promises lightly.

"Listen up, kiddies!"

Entering the locker room two steps in front of our do-gooder counselor was the pool counselor. He was of the community service variety and his eyes told us he was not above dragging one of us behind the building for a proper beating if he surmised we deserved it.

"I want everybody to pick a buddy for the pool. And when I blow this whistle, no matter what's going on, no matter what you're doing, I don't care if you're half way down from the high dive, you find your buddy and grab hold of him. This way I know if anybody drowned. I blow this whistle and you don't stop and grab your buddy, I'm gonna drown you myself. We understand each other?"

A half-hearted chorus of "yeahs" rose up from the newly minted Ojibwas.

"I can't hear you!"

"YEAH!" cried out our tribe, eager to get to the damn pool.

"All right, buddy up."

He blew his whistle and the locker room was reduced to chaos as the all-important task of picking a pool buddy commenced. I looked to Frank, but he was overrun with suitors and was in the process of joining forces with the big kid who hassled our group counselor. My eyes quickly surveyed the rest of our tribe. They were buddying up all around me and I was frozen in place. Ten seconds had ticked off the clock, which is nothing short of a millennium in adolescent buddy choosing and I was still standing alone. I was convinced I'd be left buddy-less when I felt someone tug my arm. I looked over to see a pair of saliva-soaked braces flapping a mile a minute like a hummingbird's wings.

"Let's buddy up before we get stuck with a couple of spazzes. The big chicks are already at the pool and some of them got knockers out to here."

He cupped his hands over his chest to indicate breasts the size of watermelons.

"Whatdaya say?"

"Okay."

"Hurry up then. I wanna get out there and start the long-awaited knocker hunt of the summer of '69."

In a rush to pull up his shorts, he tangled his right leg in his underpants, lost his balance, and toppled over one of the benches. Unfazed, he popped to his feet and smiled the smile of the recently hormone'd.

"I swear to god some of those freakin' knockers are out to here."

Then a high-pitched voice rang out from the far side of the locker room.

"Forget it. I'm not being his buddy."

The boy filing the protest was a heavyset kid with an accent more Queens than Bronx. He was closer to my age than Frank's, and did not have an ounce of athletic ability hiding inside his round, pasty frame. It was my experience such a boy would generally be grateful for a buddy, any buddy. Such was the nature of schoolyard politics, which I assumed transferred to summer camp. Then I saw where he was pointing. At Nelson. The only black Ojibwa. Somehow he'd managed to stay out of sight since we arrived at Silver Birch. I didn't even notice him when our tribe was formed. But with instructions to buddy up for the pool, there was no longer a place to hide.

"I ain't bein' his buddy neither," Nelson stated with heartfelt conviction as every eye in the room held fixed upon him.

"Good, 'cause I ain't bein' your buddy neither, too," the heavyset kid confirmed.

"Good, 'cause I don't want you to be my buddy."

"I wouldn't buddy with him. No way, no how," my buddy whispered in my ear.

The pool counselor yelled over the noise as he stormed from the utility closet, which was operating as his office.

"What the hell's goin' on in here? Why aren't you gettin' ready?"

The heavyset kid spoke first.

"I ain't bein' his buddy, I ain't grabbin' hold of him when the whistle blows."

"I ain't grabbin' him neither."

The counselor looked at the two boycotters, then turned to survey the rest of us.

"Who'll buddy up with him?"

He pointed at Nelson and cast his eyes around the room. There was dead silence amongst the all-white Ojibwa tribe.

"Come on, who'll buddy with him?"

Still nothing. I looked at Nelson and I could see it was as though the silence was a hand which slapped him across the face.

"I don't want to buddy with none of them," said Nelson.

The pool counselor had enough of the squabble and bore his focus into Nelson and the heavyset kid.

"Enough of this bullcrap. You two have to buddy up, that's all there is to it."

But that wasn't all there was to it. Nelson and the heavy set kid dug in their heels.

"I ain't buddyin' with him."

"And I ain't buddyin' with him."

"Fine, than neither one of you is goin' to the pool." He blew his whistle.

"Everybody get the hell out!"

At first no one moved. We were all still enthralled by the battle of wills playing out in our locker room. So the pool counselor released a second blast from the whistle, which nearly burst our eardrums.

"I said move your damn assess, now!"

The Ojibwas charged from the dank locker room as Nelson and the heavyset kid took off their shorts and pulled on their play pants. I paused a moment, watching both of them sit quietly on the edge of separate benches.

"I'd sit there all day before I'd buddy with a nigger," my buddy assured me.

I'd heard the word before. Many times, in fact. But always regarding some nameless group of people out there somewhere. People outside a moving car. Or on the television. Away from where the word was uttered. This was different. This time the word had a face to it. The boy in question, the target of the insult, was right in front of me. He pretended he didn't hear it, but I knew he did. I could see the discomfort in his eyes. The dryness of his mouth. The fear in his heart. The desire to be anywhere other than where he now sat.

Somewhere inside of me I could hear a voice. It said, "Do something. Do something." But I pushed it down. Pushed it deep within me until the voice grew softer and softer and finally disappeared. I was not yet ready to hear it.

My buddy grabbed my arm and pulled me toward the exit as he gave me my final instructions for the pool.

"Now remember to holler out when you see a set of big knockers and I'll do the same. Whoever spots the most knockers wins."

And out we went into the blistering sun leaving the darkness and the two boys behind.

When the church bell located across the street from Silver Birch's main parking lot tolled five o'clock, the Ojibwa, the Pawnee, the Apache, the Cherokee, and a litany of other Indian tribes were busy boarding busses headed for home.

I was at a dead run following Frank, who led me from bus to bus. He'd take a quick look inside, then keep moving. I presumed he was searching for the perfect bus.

"This one."

He stopped outside a red bus filled with kids from our group.

"This isn't the bus we came on."

"Duh. We're not taking our bus, pea-brain. We'll ride this one to the end, then come back here."

Frank banged on the bus doors and bellowed.

"Hey, open up."

"Why are we doin' that?" I asked.

"Cause when we don't show up everyone'll think we're gone and crap the floor."

The doors swung open. Frank ran up the steps and disappeared into the rear of the bus. I hesitated, trying to think this through. It was one thing to plan a run-away while lying in the comfort of your bed, it was another to actually go through with it out on the streets.

"Hey kid, you comin' or not? I'm not sittin' here all day," the driver mumbled.

He was young. In his early twenties. With long greasy hair held in place by a bandana and a five-day growth covering bad skin he'd decided needed a few tattoos.

Frank stuck his head out one of the windows.

"You want to move to Jersey, numb-nuts?"

As he belted out that warning, I noticed the word written across the top panel of the bus just above Frank's head. Manhattan.

"I'm outta here," said the driver.

He started to close the doors, but I stuck my arm between them before they could lock me out. I climbed the two steps, passed the driver without a look, and found Frank amongst the rest of the Ojibwa nation.

By the time we made our tenth stop at the north end of the Upper West Side, the once full bus was nearly empty. For twenty minutes I'd been staring out the window, transfixed by a part of the city I had never seen before. Manhattan was the far side of the moon to us. It wasn't a place we needed to go. If we wanted the park, we went to Van Cortland, not Central. If we wanted to swim, we didn't go to the East River, we went to City Island. If we wanted to see baseball, well, there was no baseball in Manhattan. The Yankees played in the Bronx.

On Ninety-Eighth Street, the bus stopped and two Ojibwa got off. As they walked past the driver, I noticed him sip from a bottle he had wrapped in a paper bag. He hid the bottle under his seat, lit a cigarette and closed the doors.

We continued traveling north. Faster. Our driver had increased his speed as we crossed over One Hundred Tenth Street the way a corral horse picks up his pace when he turns back for the barn and a nice portion of hay.

"Last stop," he called over his shoulder, allowing the words to drift to the ceiling in a cloud of smoke and nicotine.

That's when I realized there were only three of us left on the bus. Frank, me, and Nelson. One more stop, and it's where the black kid gets off.

I watched with trepidation as the neighborhood changed all around us. Just like the detour route we took the last day of school. But there was a difference. This place was truly frightening. The neighborhood we drove through in the Bronx, while different from what I'd known, felt like a neighborhood. This did not. It did not look like a place people could live. The buildings were too big and falling apart, the streets were too crowded, and the noise was too loud. The smells were too foreign. And there was something else rising off these streets that had me shifting in my seat, moving ever so slightly away from the glass. There was desperation. And there was anger. I could feel it. And like a lid rattling over a boiling pot, I knew it could blow off at a moment's notice. And when it did, I wanted to be far, far away.

"Jesus. Look at all of 'em out there," I heard Frank whisper under his breath.

I *was* looking at all of them out there. Because the sidewalks, as far as I could see in either direction, were filled with people, and all of them black. It no longer looked like New York. At least not the New York I knew. I wondered just how far we'd gone. How many miles must one travel to get to a place like this? And thank god there's a wide river between it and where I live.

When the bus stopped, I thought my heart would stop along with it. I sat motionless when Nelson walked slowly past me, glancing at me for just a second as he made his way toward the exit. He jumped down from the last step and was gone, vanishing into a sea of darkness. I was glad to see him go. Glad he was getting off the bus so we could close the doors, leave this neighborhood behind, and get back to the camp. But the doors didn't close. We sat motionless. And then we sat there some more. I saw Frank about to say something when a woman climbed aboard. A young black woman wearing less clothes than any woman I ever recall seeing in public. She whispered something to the driver, nibbled his ear, then licked his chin as he slipped a twenty dollar bill in the band of her short shorts and pressed his face between her emerging breasts.

I watched dumbfounded when I heard her voice.

"Looks like we got company."

My eyes shot from the woman's cleavage to her face and I realized she was looking directly at Frank and me.

I could hear my heart thumping as the driver, with his hands still grasping the sides of the woman's breasts, called out to us.

"This is the last stop."

We didn't move. We didn't speak and we didn't fully comprehend what he was telling us.

The driver released the breasts and took a short draw on his bottle.

"Well, get off."

"This isn't where we got on," Frank replied.

"But it's where you're getting off."

Frank glanced out the window. At all the people.

"We can't get off here."

"I gotta drop this bus at the garage and then I got stuff to do. So you're gettin' off."

"Are you nuts? Look at 'em out there. They'll chop us to pieces."

"Ain't no one gonna chop your little white ass to pieces," the woman said.

"Come on, hit the road." The driver insisted.

"You can't just drop us anywhere," Frank argued. "You're supposed to take us back to the camp."

"No, you're supposed to get off at the right stop, smart guy. And I ain't drivin' all the way back to freakin' New Jersey 'cause you two got your asses screwed on backwards. So just back track yourselves down Broadway till you find your stop."

Frank didn't speak, but he didn't budge either.

"I'm not gonna ask again."

"Then don't."

The woman laughed and her whole body jiggled when she did.

"Boy's got some sand. I'll give 'im that."

She then smiled at Frank.

"You got any money in your pocket, honey buns?"

The driver rose from his seat.

"If that's the way you wanna play it, fine by me."

He started coming toward us when Frank shouted.

"All right!"

The driver stopped. Frank grabbed hold of me and pulled me from my seat. Then, slowly, we walked toward the front of the bus. We moved past the driver, past the barely-dressed woman, past the last bastion of safety. We paused at the doors, which were still open and looked out at an angry, dangerous world.

"Back down Broadway. You'll find your stop."

Frank went first, and the two of us exited the bus onto the sidewalk. My foot had barely touched the pavement when Frank turned sharply toward the bus and shrieked at the driver, who had returned to his seat.

"I hope you crash and break all your bones and burn to death screaming and yelling with your head cut off in a pile of guts!"

The driver looked at Frank, laughed, then shut the doors and drove away leaving us in a dark ocean of people who scared us to death.

"What are we gonna do?" I said.

"I don't know." Frank whispered as we looked through the crowd for a white face.

"I don't know."

Chapter *Four*

My mother had been widowed a mere seven months, her husband shot down in a coffee shop, and now she was about to learn her sons were missing. My brother and I had not considered the totality of those circumstances when we woke that morning. We didn't posses the capacity, or desire, to see beyond our own needs and wants. So often we are unaware of the connectivity which binds each of us one to the other. Perhaps because at times we wish it didn't exist. But no depth of independence, no state of isolation, no self-made wall, however thick, can sever the bind between a mother and her children. And while that connective force is built with love and joy, it is equally capable of carrying with it pain and suffering.

My mother spoke of this day often, and when she did the details of what was said, what was felt, what was lived, never varied. Even when decades separated the telling of it. And as such, it became part of my memory, my reality, and I cannot convey the full breadth of this story without including the day as lived by my mother.

True to her word, my mother stood on the sidewalk in front of our house when the black and grey bus chugged to a stop at precisely six o'clock. It had been a long day. A nervous day. A day spent fidgeting behind the desk she occupied in the secretary pool of the Bell Telephone Company. From the moment she punched in at eight o'clock a.m., she had begun counting down the hours. Spending her time wondering how my brother and I made out, if we had fun. Wondering if the tension between her and me had been dissipated by a long swim and a horseback ride through the woodlands of New Jersey.

She took a deep breath, pushed down her emotions and smiled as the old driver opened the doors of the creaky bus. But nothing happened. Her boys did not come bounding down the steps. They did not wrap their sunburned arms around her neck. They did not stumble over words as they leapt into stories of the day's adventures. She waited, then waited some more.

"Frank? Mickey?"

Another twenty seconds went by, but neither of her sons exited the bus.

"Very funny."

She stepped from the curb and took position just outside the doors.

"Come on, guys, off the bus chop chop. I've got dinner in the oven."

Nothing. She heard the driver sigh impatiently before hollering toward the rear of the vehicle.

"You're making me late, let's go."

He then looked down at my mother, who, growing self-conscious, rolled her eyes and forced a smile.

"I'm serious now, get off the bus," she called out.

Still nothing. The first hint of anxiety stung her skin like a mosquito. It carried just enough bite to let her know it was there, but not so much as to draw her full attention. So she swatted it away and continued.

"I'm counting to ten and you better be out here standing right beside me when I'm done."

She heard snickering from inside the bus as every youngster aboard began counting in mock unison.

"One, two, three . . ."

Forget what you've heard about a woman scorned. A woman mocked is the most dangerous creature on the planet and my mother charged the steps loaded for bear.

"That's enough!"

Everyone went quiet, including the driver.

"Now you two get off this bus right now."

Her jaw was set, but her sons did not rise up to make themselves known.

"All right, that tears it."

Fully prepared to grab our ears and drag us from the bus, my mother stormed down the aisle and checked every nook and cranny. She looked into the faces, under the seats, under the clothes but found nothing. The anxiety now hit her like a tidal wave. Her skin went cold. Her mind burned. And the ground fell out from under her feet.

"Oh god."

She spun hard and bore her eyes into the driver who felt the full force of their gaze.

"Where the hell are my kids?!"

Frank and I pushed up against a graffiti-covered wall to avoid being trampled by the foot traffic, which seemed to have no pause, let alone end. People moved like a river with currents flowing in all directions. Tall people, short people. Fat people, skinny people. Old, young, sick, healthy, and all of them black.

It may have been life as usual in this part of the city, but that's not how it looked to me, not as the sun sat low in the sky and shadows crept like alley cats across the sidewalk. The whole place took on an eerie quality. The scars on the buildings, the holes of neglect in the roads, the worn out cars, the forgotten playgrounds, and the people. All those people. Towering over two boys not yet nine years old.

"Look at 'em," I whispered to Frank so as not to be heard by anyone but him. "There's tons of them. We're the only ones here. There's nobody here but them."

"We gotta get out of here," Frank said.

"They're gonna kill us."

"No, they're not."

"You said they would. Said they'd chop us up."

A hand landed on my shoulder and froze me in my place.

"You lost?"

It was an older woman. With the kind of meaty arms one develops from doing heavy work over a long period of time.

"I said, is you boys lost?" She repeated while pushing a set of thick glasses up the bridge of her nose.

I saw Frank's mouth begin to open and I took off like a shot. I ran as hard as I could. Not knowing where I was going. Just running. My heart was pounding, my lungs filling with hot air as I weaved in and out of the bodies clogging the street. My eyes were wide and the heat in my face brought sweat to my brow, but I kept running.

"Mickey!"

I heard Frank calling my name, but I couldn't stop. My body was moving on adrenalin. I was scared, and fear shuts off the brain, erasing reason and thought so all you're left with is instinct, and mine said run.

"Mickey, goddamnit!"

I reached the end of the sidewalk and shot across One Hundred Thirtieth Street, which sent horns blaring and cars swerving in all directions.

I reached the opposite side of the intersection at a full run and slammed into something hard. Something which shot me back three feet and put me flat on my butt. I tried to get up as quickly as I could, but I was dazed and fell back to my side. Then I heard a voice. Deep and gruff, with the slightest hint of a rural accent, perhaps somewhere down south.

"Where's your damn dog?"

I looked up and saw a black man of sixty, maybe more. He was solid. A mountain. From behind, you might think he was young, in the prime condition of his life. But from the front his face told another story. The lines were etched deep and looked as if they told painful stories. About his feet were small broken bottles and the growing stains of water-based paint. His enormous hand reached out, grabbed hold of my shirt, and lifted me like I was a bag of feathers.

"I said, where's your damn dog?"

He placed me on my feet and I managed to produce some sort of answer.

"There's no dog," I stammered.

"Well, you're blind, ain't ya?"

I was confused and frightened, which made it impossible to think or speak.

"Ain't ya, I says?"

"No."

"Well, if you ain't blind, what the hell's wrong with you? You just stupid? Somethin' not right upstairs?"

I could feel my body begin to vibrate as fear grabbed hold of me with both hands.

"Ya nearly got yourself killed crossin' that street. You know that, dontcha?"

His eyes held fire and I braced myself for the physical assault I expected to rain down upon me.

"What're you deaf and blind? Answer me, boy."

"I'm sorry."

"Sorry? Sorry ain't a big eraser. Sorry ain't gonna do me no good with a busted back. Or you with a tire from a two-thousand pound Buick Riviera sittin' on your flattened skull. Is it?"

"No."

"That's right. And who's gonna pay for my paints? You? I don't think so. I think I'm gonna have to pay for somethin' you done."

His eyes weren't bloodshot, but the whites were milky and crisscrossed with thin strands of red.

"Does that sound fair to you?"

"No."

"Me neither. But there it is."

He stood a moment longer, then turned his eyes to his broken paints, picked up three small brushes no bigger than pencils, and slid them into his pocket.

"Cost me near nine dollars. You ain't got nine dollars, do ya?"

"No."

"Didn't think so. Didn't think so at all."

He took one last look at me, and moved on, disappearing into the crowd of black faces.

I took my first breath as Frank ran up beside me and pulled me into the door way of an empty storefront.

"Ya dumb nut. Lucky he didn't beat the crap out of you. What the hell were you runnin' for?"

"You were gonna talk to that lady."

"I was not."

"Ma said never talk to strangers and you were gonna talk to her!"

"I was not!"

"Were too. You were gonna talk to her and tell her everything!"

"I wasn't gonna tell her nothin'!"

Tears began rolling down my cheeks. I felt the world close in around me.

"Don't start cryin', " Frank said in a calmer voice. "They'll start looking at us for sure if you start cryin'."

The tears just came harder.

"What are we gonna do?" I cried, my voice breaking from the stress.

Frank could see my limbs begin to tremble, and it scared him more than the place we were in.

"We'll call home. We'll call home and mom'll come get us."

"How's she gonna know where to come if we don't know where we are?"

"She'll know where we are. It'll be okay."

Frank's certainty, real or not, was a comfort, and I managed to pull myself together as best I could. I wiped the last of the tears from my cheeks and dried my hands on my shirt.

"I spent all my money at camp," Frank said. "You got any money left?"

"The dollar Ma gave me."

"The whole dollar?"

"Yeah."

"Didn't you buy no lunch?"

"I had to go to the bathroom and the toilet paper was all wet. So I used my underwear 'cause it got messy and by the time I got back they didn't have anything left 'cept the lima beans and the jello so the . . ."

"All right already," Frank said. "Just give me the damn dollar."

I reached into my pants pocket, fished out the dollar, and held it up. Frank snatched it from my hand and buried it in his pocket.

"Don't pull it out like it's the freakin' American flag. They'll take it off us fast as a fart."

"Sorry."

"All right. We gotta get change."

We looked through the continuous foot traffic and searched for a place where we might turn a dollar into dimes. There weren't many, not that we could see. None of the shops and none of the people looked inviting. Far from it. I was about to give up when I saw him. Across the street, standing in front of a fenced-off lot. A white man.

"Look," I said, pointing.

Frank followed my finger and caught sight of a white man, about forty, and thin as a piece of straw.

"Come on."

Frank gave me a tug on the arm and I followed him to the intersection.

"Wait for the light."

In a few seconds it turned green and we hustled across as quickly as we could. We closed distance in no time and steadied our step as we approached our savior.

"Let me do the talkin'," Frank ordered.

We got within a few feet of the man, who I now noticed was leaning against the fence as though his muscles had all turned to mush. He was wearing old, faded jeans, a tie-dyed t-shirt, and some kind of leather hat that looked to have lost its shape years before.

"You got change of a dollar?"

The man's eyes were open, but Frank's question seemed to wake him from a nap. He slowly wiped his face and I noticed he wore rings on every single finger of each hand, even the thumbs. He looked over and smiled, revealing a mouth that had lost several of its residents. He cleared his throat.

"You got a dollar?"

"Yeah." I said.

"I'm doin' the talkin'," Frank barked.

He turned back to the man and looked him up and down before repeating his question.

"Well, you got the change or not?"

"Let me see the dollar," the man said.

"Let me see the change," Frank countered.

The man swayed, laughed, and stomped his foot with amusement.

"Smart kid. Can't be too careful in this neighborhood, if you know what I mean."

Then he got serious. Motioned us close and lowered his voice like he was telling us a secret.

"Truth is, I don't carry that much change on me. What with thieves and all runnin' around here thick as lice. But I can get it for you. Of course I'll want a dime for my troubles. I mean, ten percent is the standard rate. But you look like someone who already knows that?"

"Yeah, I know it," Frank lied. "Dime's fair."

"Cool. Just give me the buck and I'll meet you back here in five minutes."

Frank hesitated.

"Hey, you can ask somebody else if you want to. I'm just tryin' to help."

"Give it to him," I said.

"I'm doin' this," Frank reminded me.

 Frank look around at all the black faces on the street, then pulled the dollar from his pocket.

"Five minutes?" Frank asked.

"Maybe less."

Frank handed over the dollar.

"Make sure you don't go nowhere 'cause I don't wanna be carryin' that kind of money on me, if you know what I mean."

"We won't go anywhere," I said.

"Good. See you in five."

"Or less," Frank added.

"Or less."

The guy tipped his leather hat and vanished.

I turned to Frank.

"That was lucky."

"Yeah."

Chapter Five

The one phone we kept in our home rested on a small table tucked in a nook just off the foyer. My mother stood over it ignoring the chair she inherited from her Aunt Nettie, just like she was ignoring the bell from the timer letting her know the meatloaf was finished cooking in the oven. She was in a panic. At first she wouldn't get off the bus, didn't want the driver leaving. It didn't make much sense, but that didn't matter. Her children were missing and she needed something to hold on to. Eventually the driver convinced her the best course of action was for him to drop off the rest of the kids and return to the camp to see if we were there.

When she entered our house, she walked in circles, trying to get her mind to slow, to be useful. It took time, but she finally realized the obvious. Call the camp. She had the number written on a notepad beside the phone and dialed. But no one picked up. It just rang and rang. Such was the manner of phone usage in the age before voicemail and answering machines. But the action served to steady her nerves. Clear thought was more forthcoming. Still, she wanted help, she didn't want to be alone. To be alone was to be without her missing children and that was too much. So she now stood over the table searching the address book for Santangelo Trucking. But even after she found the number, it took three attempts to dial it correctly, as her hand was trembling. Finally the call was made and a voice picked up on the other end of the line.

"Santangelo Trucking."

"I'd like to speak to Patrick O'Neil please."

"Who's calling?"

"His sister-in-law."

"Hold the line."

Music came across the wire. A soft, instrumental piece designed to keep the caller calm. It failed. The slow melody only served to heighten my mother's anxiety and increase her desire to speak with my Uncle Pat sooner rather than later.

"I'm sorry, he's out in the field."

"Can't you call him in the truck?"

"I'm sorry, but we . . ."

"Just call him, please!"

"As I was saying, we . . ."

"This is an emergency, a family emergency, and I need to speak with him now."

"I understand, but . . ."

"Goddamnit, my children are missing!"

And with those words, spoken aloud for the first time, came a flood of tears and the agony of a mother with missing children.

Frank and I had barely said a word since the white man took off with our dollar. We kept huddled against the fence, away from the foot traffic and the dangers of the world less than ten feet away. But the sun was almost down and that meant trouble.

"He ain't comin' back." Frank said.

"You don't know that."

"It's been a half hour. He ain't comin'."

"Maybe he couldn't find change."

"And maybe I'm gonna grow broccoli outta the top of my head."

We stood looking out at the seething city before us. At the stripped car halfway up the sidewalk, at the homeless man scrounging food from a garbage can, at the streetlamp that began to flicker then suddenly burn out, taking the light with it.

"I knew we shouldn't have given' it to him," Frank said. "I told you to keep your mouth shut."

"You're the one who gave it to him."

"You're the one who said to give it to him. I was thinkin' it over and woulda probably said no, but you said give it to him."

"Who said you had to listen?"

"Just shut up."

Frank was getting angry because he was getting scared.

"It's almost dark. When it's fully dark we're good and screwed."

"What are we gonna do?"

"We gotta call Ma."

"How we gonna call Ma? We don't have any dimes."

Frank gave it some thought.

"Give me that silver dollar you got."

"No."

"Mickey, we gotta call Ma."

"Dad gave me it."

"I know, but this is an emergency."

"I don't care."

"We don't call Ma, who knows what's gonna happen. We'll probably get killed."

"You said we weren't gonna get killed."

"I was lyin' so you wouldn't get scared. But we will get killed if we don't call Ma. Then what good is that coin gonna do ya?"

"I'm keepin' it."

"Give me the damn coin."

"No."

"Gimme it."

Frank pushed me against the fence and drove his hand into my pocket, but I managed to trap the coin with my own.

"NO!"

"Would you shut up?!"

"NOOOOO!"

Eighteen months difference doesn't matter so much when you're beyond twenty years of age, but the difference between seven and eight-and-a-half is enormous. On any given day Frank could beat me from pillar to post and on several occasions did just that. He never hit me in the face, mind you. That was another of our rules of combat, no punching above the shoulders. We incorporated this regulation several years earlier because we recognized it was disrespectful to hit one's kin in the face and because we knew if my father came home and spotted bruises on our chins, cheeks or eyes a spanking would ensue which would prevent us from sitting comfortably for several days.

But this was different. Frank was trying to get my coin. He may have had the best intentions, but as they say, "The road to Hell is paved with good intentions." And Hell is what Frank got. I kicked and punched and fought like a demon until I brought the whole affair to a screeching and immediate halt with one hard bite into his forearm.

"AHHHHHHHHH! Let go!"

Certain he got the message, I removed my teeth from his skin. Frank, flustered and frantic, looked at the bite mark in his arm, then grabbed hold of my shirt just below my neck.

"You're gonna get it for that."

Frank cocked his fist and was on the precipice of driving it through my face, rules or no rules.

"Dad gave me it."

He stopped, unfurled his fist and let go of my shirt. He stared at me, then looked down at his arm and rubbed his hand over the bite.

"Better not get rabies."

In the time it took us to work out the issue of my coin, the sun had dropped out of sight. You can watch the sun all day, kill off any number of hours following it across the sky, but once it gets within two inches of the horizon a trap door opens beneath it and it falls into oblivion. And when it leaves, darkness comes.

"What are we gonna do?" I asked.

"Is that all you know how to say? 'Cause if it is, better you say nothin' at all."

So I didn't.

Frank, still scared and still pissed about his arm, looked around for an answer. We needed to do something, anything. He looked and looked and finally set his eyes on an old coffee shop across the street.

"We'll get dimes in there."

He turned to me with purpose.

"Stay close. If one of them snatches you, it's over. Like gettin' in a car."

I nodded, then followed him across the busy intersection, struggling to not to get separated by the army of people crossing with us.

Standing on the sidewalk out of the flow of pedestrians, we tried to look inside the shop, but the windows had all been painted black. Neither of us liked going in blind, but we had to get dimes, and desperate times call for desperate measures.

We approached the door and Frank whispered, "Don't say nothin'."

They say a book cannot be judged by its cover. And I admit there are places and things where the outer casing does not represent the beauty waiting inside. The oyster and the pearl come to mind. It's a lovely surprise and reminds us to always keep hope close at hand. But there are other times when the book and the cover are one and the same. The port-a-potties lining the street during the San Gennaro Feast are such items. You know what you're going to get the moment you see them and you are, in fact, correct. This coffee shop was a port-a-potty, though not as full. The seats were torn, the walls were yellow, the floors appeared to have chicken pox and the air was permanently stained with the odor of cheap cigarettes. But what caught my attention first was the sign.

Directly in front of us, nailed to an exposed support beam, was a small section of broken blackboard that I'm certain once lived in a nearby school. Scrawled across the slate in white chalk was, "Baby-backs, all you can eat."

"Jesus." I heard Frank mutter.

"Jesus." I agreed.

There was only one person sitting in the section dedicated to tables and booths. One. And it was the old man whose paints I'd broken. He sat filling up one entire side of a green vinyl booth. And in complete defiance of the laws of physics, he seemed even bigger sitting than standing. I couldn't take my eyes off him or the large plate of bones on his table. He picked one up, sucked a strand of meat from between his teeth, then mashed down into the small, sauce-covered cartilage with a sickening crunch.

"He's eatin' babies' backs," I whispered in complete horror.

We watched him chew and swallow, then we heard a clang ring out to our left. We turned and caught sight of a middle-aged man in a postal uniform tossing coins onto the counter. He got off his stool, grabbed his mail sack, and crossed to the door, taking a moment to study Frank and me as if we were exhibits in a zoo.

My eyes turned back to the man eating the babies' backs, but Frank's turned to the coins, one of which was still spinning like a top.

"Come on." Frank whispered.

"No."

I knew what he was thinking and I didn't like it one bit.

"You wanna be stuck here at night?"

"No."

"All right then."

Frank and I moved extra slowly toward the counter. If it took as long as it felt, I would have been in my seventies by the time we reached those coins.

Frank looked around and, certain the coast was clear, put his hand on the counter-top, allowing his palm to cover the coins. With his other hand, he removed a napkin from a dispenser and held it out.

"Blow your nose."

"I don't gotta blow."

Frank shoved the napkin in my hand.

"Just blow the damn thing."

I put the napkin to my nose and let out a loud, healthy honk as Frank slid the money off the counter.

"Let's go."

We turned and just as slowly made our way toward the door. There was a pay phone to our left but I suppose Frank thought he'd be tempting fate if we used the coins in the same location from which they were stolen. So we kept moving, until a hand fell upon Frank and spun him around. Towering over us was the cook, who had quietly come from the kitchen.

"What the hell you think you're doing?"

"I didn't do nothin'," Frank replied.

"You think I didn't see that? You think I'm an idiot? That what you're sayin'?"

"He didn't take nothin'," I said.

"That so?"

The cook squeezed Frank's hand and the coins fell to the floor.

"You're gonna get your ass whooped now."

The cook dragged Frank, kicking and yelling, to an empty table.

"Let go of me!"

"Too late." The cook said as he pushed Frank over the table-top. "You're gonna pay for your crimes."

I wanted to help, but I didn't know what to do. I could feel myself shutting down. Pulling in my antennae. I wanted to do something, but all I could do was tremble.

"We just wanted to call our mom," Frank pleaded.

But the cook was unmoved. He raised up his thick hand and brought it down on Frank's rear with a loud, hard thwack. Frank cried out, but the cook didn't stop. He hit Frank again and again.

"Please." It was all I could say, all I could manage to get out of my mouth.

It had no effect and the cook continued with his assault. He hit Frank a fourth time and a fifth, but when he raised his hand for the sixth, someone grabbed it. It was the man with the broken paints.

"Boy just wanted to call his Mama."

"Ain't none of your business. Little peckerwood was stealin' my money. What I look like, the goddamn Chase Manhattan Bank?"

The cook, who was half the older man's age, tried to wrench his hand free, but he couldn't.

"Boy just wanted to call his Mama."

The older man looked hard into the cook's eyes. And when that look finished saying all it had to say, he turned to me.

"Pick up them coins."

I was too frightened to move. I stood staring.

"Go on."

Somehow I got my body to move and quickly picked the coins off the floor.

"Now put 'em back on the counter where you found 'em."

I followed his instruction as the older man turned to the cook.

"Now let the boy up."

The cook held is grasp a moment longer then let go of Frank, who pulled away seething in anger.

"Boy deserves a whoopin'."

"You deserve it!" Frank barked, eyes flooded with tears. "If my father was here he'd shoot you dead."

"Shut your mouth." The older man ordered.

"See what I'm sayin'?" The cook said. "That who you wanna help?"

"Just get your money and get back in the kitchen." The older man replied.

The cook grabbed the coins off the counter and stomped into the kitchen.

The old man looked at Frank.

"Need some change to call your Mama, should just ask for it. Ain't nothin' worse than a thief. Can't ever trust 'em after they done stole. Not for a hundred years."

He slid one of his large hands into his pocket.

"Where're you boys from?"

We didn't answer him.

"I ain't gonna know how much you need for the call if I don't know where you're callin' to."

I was waiting for Frank to do the talking, but he wasn't saying a word. Something had been taken out of him by that cook, by being pushed over a table-top like an animal. And now he was sticking to the rules. No talking to strangers. Not a word. No matter what.

"Suit yourself."

The old man turned and started back toward his booth when words jumped from my mouth.

"The Bronx."

"Mickey!"

The old man stopped and turned. "Mickey, huh? After Mantle I bet?"

"Yeah."

He looked at Frank. "So who you named after, DiMaggio? You a Joe?"

"I ain't tellin'. I don't talk to strangers."

"Especially no colored one," said the old man.

He eyeballed Frank, then turned to me as he pulled his hand from his pocket.

"It'll cost you twenty cents to call the Bronx from here. So that makes nine ten you owe me includin' the paints you done busted all over the sidewalk."

He handed me two dimes and went back to his bones.

Frank grabbed the coins and ducked into the phone booth. He lifted the receiver, then stopped and came back out.

"Where's here?"

The old man picked up a baby back and didn't let his eyes move toward Frank one iota.

"I don't talk to no strangers neither. Especially white ones."

Frank swallowed his pride and his anger.

"Frank."

"Not after Robinson, I'm wagerin'."

The old man bit down on the bone.

"You're in Harlem, Frank. Address is on a sticker at the base of the phone."

Frank grabbed my arm and pulled me into the phone booth and shut the door behind us. He dropped the two dimes into the machine and began to dial.

"Think she's gonna be mad?" I asked.

"Yeah."

Then Frank hung up.

"What?"

"It's busy."

"Why?"

"Whatdaya mean, why? 'Cause someone's usin' it. Ma's probably callin' for us. We gotta wait a few seconds, then call back."

Frank counted ten, then dropped the coins back into the phone and dialed.

"It's still busy."

"How much longer is she gonna be on the phone?"

"Six minutes and twelve seconds. How the hell am I supposed to know?"

We stood waiting in loud silence.

"She could be on forever." I said.

"She's not gonna be on forever."

"You don't know. You just said, how am I supposed to know."

"You are really getting on my last . . ." Frank stopped and sniffed the air, which wasn't good.

"Did you fart?"

"I got nervous and couldn't hold it."

"Jeez, Mick. Get outta here, you're meltin' my eyeballs."

"No."

"Yes."

"No . . ."

Frank swung open the phone booth door and pushed me into the shop. I tried to get back in, but he was holding the door shut. So I stood with my back against the wall and watched the old man down a glass of soda and wipe his sauce covered hands on a napkin.

"What're you lookin' at?" he asked.

I just shook my head and watched him pick up another rib.

"Never seen a colored man before? That it?"

"Not this close."

"Two ears, two eyes, same as you."

He bit into his food and tried to chew in peace, but I suspect he could feel me staring at him.

"You ain't eaten, have ya?"

I shook my head again.

"Every time a colored man gets around a white man it costs him somethin'. Well, come on."

I didn't move.

"This hog ain't gonna walk across the floor."

"That's a hog?"

"What did you think it was?"

I glanced at the words written on the broken piece of blackboard.

"A baby's back."

"A what? For crissakes boy, you think I'm sittin' here pretty as you please eaten a goddamn baby? What the hell's the matter with you? Where'd you get an idea like that?"

"Tommy Gorman's father said in Africa the big ones eat the little ones."

"Well, Tommy Gorman's father is an idiot. And this here was a pig. They just call 'em baby backs on account they small." He shook his head in disbelief. "Eatin' babies. Ain't you got a brain in that head?"

I nodded.

"Then use it." The old man put down his drink and waved me over. "Come on."

I crossed toward the table and stood at its edge, staring at the ribs.

"They ain't gonna bite you."

I reached into the plate and grabbed one. I was still scared, but I was starving and hunger is a powerful motivator. I even slid into the booth opposite the old man, taking a seat as I chewed on the tangy baby back.

"Good, ain't they?"

"Yeah."

"These here are wet rub. I like dry rub but they don't do it like that up north."

"It's still busy," I heard Frank say as he stepped from the phone booth and caught sight of me.

"What the hell're you doin'?"

"It's okay, they ain't babies, they're pig."

"You want some?" The old man offered.

Frank was hungry, but he wasn't about to take food from a stranger.

"Well, if you ain't gonna eat, get back in the phone booth. You're given me the willies watchin' us like some damn buzzard."

The old man went back to chewing and Frank went back into the phone booth. After a moment, the old man cleared his throat and caught my eyes with his.

"Name's Jack. Jack Hutchins."

"Mickey O'Neil. My brother's Frank O'Neil. He's named after Gifford. My dad liked football too."

"He's a good one."

"You knew my dad?"

"What? No. Gifford. Gifford was a good one."

"Oh, yeah. He was a good one."

I took a big bite of meat and chewed like it was the last piece of food on the planet.

Jack wiped his mouth with a napkin and leaned forward in his seat.

"So, Mickey, what's two white boys doin' in Harlem?"

Chapter Six

The operator who fielded the call at Santangelo Trucking was a mother herself. She got word to my Uncle Pat, who pulled off the highway just outside of Metuchen, New Jersey and called my mother.

"Did you call the camp?"

"I called them. They don't know. Nobody knows."

"Well, what did they say?"

"They said they don't know. Christ Pat . . ."

"All right, calm down."

"Don't tell me to calm down."

"Well, getting in a panic is not gonna help."

"I'm alone here, Pat."

"I understand."

"Can't you just let somebody else finish the haul?"

"They probably just ran away 'cause of all that's happened. Soon as they're hungry, which will be any minute now, they'll be back."

"They didn't get on the bus! How the hell are they gonna get all the way back here?"

A clicking noise crept over the phone and my mother could tell Pat was gone.

"Pat? You there? What the . . ."

"Mrs. O'Neil?"

"What? Who is this?"

"This is operator 279. Is this Mrs. O'Neil?"

"Yes."

"I have a request for an emergency break in from Frank and Mickey O'Neil."

"Oh god, yes, please."

"Hold please."

My mother held the line as her eyes flooded with tears. She would often say it was the longest six seconds of her life.

"Hello," Jack said.

My mother was startled by the deep tone of the voice speaking to her.

"Who is this?"

"Would you stop crowding me. Another inch closer, you'll be half way up my ass."

Inside the coffee shop, inside the phone booth, Jack held the receiver as Frank and I pressed behind him.

"Just back up a step," Jack ordered.

We stepped back and Jack once again spoke into the phone.

"Mrs. O'Neil."

"Who is this?" My mother asked with more urgency.

"My name is Jack Hutchins. I'm with your boys."

"Oh my god. Are they okay? Who are you?" My mother fired her questions in rapid succession.

"They're okay. They got on the wrong bus is all."

"Where are they?"

"In Harlem."

"Oh my god, please don't hurt my babies. Please, I'll do anything."

"Ain't no one gonna hurt your damn babies," Jack barked. "Here, I'll put your oldest boy on the phone."

Jack handed the phone to Frank, then crossed toward the counter to pay the cook, who was trying to clean syrup from the salt and pepper shakers.

"Hello," Frank said.

"Baby, are you okay, you all right?"

"I'm okay."

"And your brother, is he okay?"

"He's okay too."

"You had me scared to death. Where are you?

"In Harlem."

"Where in Harlem?"

"In a coffee shop."

"Is Mickey next to you?

"Yeah."

"Let me talk to him."

Frank held out the phone.

"She wants to talk to you."

I traded places with Frank and spoke.

"Hello," I said.

"Hi sweetie. You okay?"

"Yeah."

"You sure?"

"Yeah."

"You're not feelin' nervous, are ya?"

"A little."

"But you're okay?"

"Yeah."

"What happened? Why didn't you call me?"

"We tried. Frank stole some money so we could call you after the white guy stole ours, but Frank got caught and the cook started to beat him and Jack stopped him and told us we were thieves and then he gave us two dimes and some ribs but it was okay 'cause they weren't from a baby."

"What?"

"They weren't from a baby."

"Is he still there?"

"Frank?"

"No, the man."

"Yeah."

"Let me talk to him."

I leaned out of the booth and caught Jack's eye.

"She wants to talk to you."

"What for?" Jack asked.

I ducked back into the phone booth.

"He wants to know what for?"

"Just tell him to please talk to me."

I leaned out a second time.

"She said to tell you, please." Then I whispered, "She's crying."

Jack eyed me, but didn't move. I stepped back into the booth.

"He doesn't want to talk to you."

"Gimme the damn phone," Jack grumbled as he reached into the booth.

I handed him the receiver and slipped behind him where Frank was still standing.

"This is Jack Hutchins."

"Uhm, where are you, I know it's a coffee shop..."

"We're at a place called Dizzy's on a Hundred Thirty-Third and Broadway. But he's closin' up. Only open for breakfast and lunch."

"Can you wait with them someplace?"

"I can't wait with them, I got things I gotta do and then I gotta get over to work."

"What about the other man who's there? The owner? Would he stay with them?"

Jack looked over at the cook, who was closing out the register.

"I don't think you want to leave them with him. I suppose you don't know anybody up around here?"

"No. Can you take them to the police station? I can meet them there?"

"I got work I gotta get to."

"Please."

"Yeah, well, I suppose I could drop 'em for ya over at the Twenty-Eighth Precinct."

He looked at Frank and me.

"Actually you don't want to have them sittin' in that place. It's not like police stations where you from. It's dangerous as can be, and they ain't gonna be able to pay no special mind to no young boys."

"I don't know what else to do," my mother said.

Jack took a deep breath and spoke into the phone.

"You're in the Bronx, right?"

"Yes."

"Well, I could take 'em with me over to work, it's in the Bronx too, and you can get 'em there."

"Where in the Bronx?"

"Yankee Stadium."

"Thank you. Thank you so much. I don't have much money but I . . ."

"I don't need none of your money. I got my own money. That what you think I'm doin' here? Tryin' to get your money?"

"No, no, I'm sorry."

"Cause I don't need some white woman decidin' for herself I took her kids to get money. You hear me? I don't need that. I'll leave 'em right here."

"No. No. I'm sorry."

"All right. Just go to the main gate when you get there and tell 'em you want Jack Hutchins in maintenance. I'll leave word you're comin'. Like I said, I got some things to do, so I'll be gettin' there round nine, so don't be late. I ain't no baby sitter."

"I won't. Thank you."

"Yeah."

"If I could talk to Frank please."

"She wants to talk to you."

Jack handed the phone to Frank.

"I just wanted to say goodbye." My mother said. "Take care of your brother. If he starts to get overly nervous, you know you gotta calm him down, right?"

"Yeah."

"Okay. Now listen to me, but don't say nothing. Don't let this man separate you and your brother. And don't let him take you anywhere alone. You hear me? You've got to stay together, and in public."

"Okay."

"I'm serious. Together, and in public."

"Yeah, okay.'

"All right. I love you."

"Love you too."

Frank hung up the phone. My mother was about to do the same when she heard that clicking noise and then my Uncle Pat.

"Hello? You there?"

"Pat?"

"What happened? I've been trying to get . . ."

"I just spoke to them."

"Are they all right?"

"Yeah. They sounded scared, but they were okay."

"Where are they, what happened?"

"They got on the wrong bus."

"So where are they?"

"In Harlem."

"Harlem?!"

"At a coffee shop called Dizzy's."

"They alone?"

"No, they're with a man who gave them some money for the call. His name is Jack Hutchins. He's taking them to Yankee Stadium."

"What the hell for? There ain't no game at Yankee Stadium today."

"He works there."

"Is he colored?"

"I suppose so, yeah."

"Jesus. You left them with a colored guy?"

"What the hell was I suppose to say? Just leave 'em alone in the street till I get there?!"

"So you're meeting him there?"

"Yeah."

"By yourself?"

"Apparently so."

Frank and I stood waiting near the door as Jack gathered his things from his booth. We could hear the phone ringing, but we didn't pay much attention to it.

"You work for the Yankees?" Frank asked.

"That's right. So I don't want no nonsense. You start pullin' nonsense and I'll dump you on the spot. 'Cause I don't care. This ain't my problem. And I ain't been late in almost thirty years and I don't plan on startin' now. You hear me? 'Cause they just lookin' for a reason to get rid of a man my age. You understand what I'm sayin' to ya?"

The cook stepped from the phone booth.

"It's for you."

"For me?" Jack said.

"That what I said. And don't be makin' it long, I wanna get outta here."

Jack crossed to the phone as the cook gave him one last piece of advice.

"And don't be takin' no private calls in here."

Jack ignored him and picked up the phone.

"Hello?"

"You Jack Hutchins?"

"Who this?"

"My name is Patrick O'Neil. Those boys you have are my brother's sons."

"Yeah?"

"Now you know me . . . and I know you. You understand what I'm sayin' to you?"

Jack took a breath.

"I understand."

"Good, 'cause I don't want any confusion."

"I'm runnin' late." Jack said.

"You go on then, Jack Hutchins. And you be sure to take care good care of those boys."

Jack heard a loud click as Uncle Pat hung up the phone. He put the handset into the cradle and stepped from the booth.

"Who was that?" Frank wanted to know.

"Your uncle."

"Did he sound mad?" I asked.

"Yeah, he sounded mad. Now I gotta pick up my stuff and get movin'."

"Where's your stuff?" Frank wanted to know.

"Where I live."

"Where do you live?"

"You writin' a book about my life? Is that it, you a writer, Frank? You work for the newspapers?"

"No."

"Then you never mind where I live."

Jack pushed open the door and the three of us stepped out into the dark, Harlem night.

"Should have my head examined cartin' 'round two white boys."

Chapter Seven

Jack Hutchins stood six feet five and one quarter inches tall and a good portion of that was legs. At least it seemed that way to Frank and me as we all but ran to keep up with his stride. Each time he put a foot forward it gobbled up over a yard of sidewalk, which was three times more territory than we could cover.

"I hope he don't live too far," Frank said.

And I couldn't have agreed more. This was going to be a blistering pace to maintain, and I could already tell Jack was not one to make allowances for the shortcomings of others. Even if that shortcoming was a question of simply being short. But there was darkness all around us and the danger we perceived was never far from hand, so I was determined, no matter what degree of sacrifice it took, to keep my legs pumping. I was not going to fall too far behind Mr. Jack Hutchins. Not when what I wanted, what I needed, existed inside an invisible circle that surrounded him, and that was safety.

Still, as Frank and I quickstepped behind Jack, I was consumed with two competing emotions. Ever since our driver tossed us from his bus onto the forbidding sidewalks of Harlem, fear and anxiety had feasted on my soul. But when Jack caught hold of the cook's hand on its way to applying another welt to Frank's butt, I began to feel lighter. Fear and anxiety are heavy emotions. I cannot prove this scientifically, but I know it to be true. And carrying around their weight can wear out your body as well as your mind. So this relief, this breath of air that filled my lungs, was welcomed with open arms. But at my center, in the place where the navigation of my being is calculated and its course charted, fear reigned.

There was the fear of the place and the people, of the darkness that dropped over the city like a velvet curtain, of whatever demon might race out from the shadows to take hold of me. But there was also the fear that Jack might dump us at a moment's notice. Decide we were not worth the trouble. Leave us to once again fend for ourselves, which we could not do. It's a frightening thing to learn you are not self-sufficient. And despite all the facts of your life which define that reality as self-evident, it comes as a complete shock to your system when you discover it to be the case. My parents provided me with a place to sleep, clothes to cover my body, food to eat, protection from evil, yet only now, only hurrying with my brother behind a man I did not know, yet could not lose, did I realize I could not take care of myself.

But that was not the fear foremost in my mind. What had me concerned was something I sensed. Something I felt emanating from Jack. It wafted off his body with a heavy scent. He was steeped in it. He had come to our aid in the coffee shop, had stepped in to speak with the operator when Frank's calls to our mother were greeted with continuous busy signals, had agreed to keep us with him and take us to Yankee Stadium to rejoin our family. But what I sensed, what I knew without question, was that Jack was filled with anger. And even at seven years of age, I knew a thing or two about anger. Anger was a mask. It did not exist on its own. It was a place where you arrived after a long, painful journey. It was the child of shame, of sadness, of grief, of omission, of any number of the world's cuts and bruises. I knew a thing or two about anger and I could see it all over Jack.

"It's really dark," I whispered to Frank as we worked to keep pace with Jack.

I was stating the obvious, but I needed to hear Frank's voice. The silence between us was louder than all the clamoring the city dished up and I wanted it broken.

"I know. If he does anything weird, just start runnin'."

"Which way?"

"Any way."

"Supposing we get separated?

"Then run the way I'm runnin'. Jesus, Mick."

We kept moving west, crossing a street three times wider than the streets back home. And we passed people, lots of people. And Jack didn't acknowledge any of them.

"I thought you said they all knew each other?"

"I said they're all related. From way back. But most of them haven't seen each other ever so they don't know it."

"That's the Puerto Ricans." Jack tossed back without turning his head. "The Puerto Ricans are all related."

He then looked at us and slowed just enough to underscore his point.

"We're the ones sneakin' round at night with long carvin' knives, eatin' our children and playin' harmonicas."

Jack stopped and opened the door to a small grocery store. "I gotta get some things."

Unlike my mom, Jack did not hold the door open and wait for Frank and me to enter first. He simply pushed inside the shop and let the door close behind him. Frank held out his hand and stopped me from entering.

"What?"

"Just wanna make sure there's other people in there."

Frank looked through the glass door and saw enough people to make him feel safe. Funny how the other black people had now become necessary to feel safe.

By the time Frank and I made our way inside Jack had a brown paper bag in hand and was trolling a narrow aisle that bordered a row of crates filled with green-looking things. I say green-looking things because I had no idea what was in those crates.

"They look like weeds," Frank said, apparently thinking the same thing.

Jack shot him a look that set Frank to scrambling.

"But I bet they taste good."

"You lose that bet." Jack answered.

He dropped a handful of weeds into his bag.

"I ain't never ate this stuff for the taste. Just keeps your heart pumpin' is all. Though I suppose some folks feel different."

Jack continued up the aisle and found myself looking at all the items offered by this shop. They were basically the same goods offered at the markets at home, just not as nice. The meats and fish looked poorly. Their color and cut was not in the least bit appetizing. The canned and boxed items were generic and packaged in bland colored materials. It was as if whoever was responsible for filling this store brought the leftovers from other stores.

Jack turned toward a wall of shelves at the back of the shop, snatched a big box of oatmeal, some loose tobacco, and a packet of rolling papers. We followed him toward the counter, where a tired looking man with an outcropping of small bumps around his eyes pulled on his glasses.

"That everything?"

"Ain't everything, but it's all I'm gettin'."

The cashier priced him out.

"Three seventy-eight."

Jack reached into his pocket for his money and when he pulled his hand out some coins went flying to the floor.

I immediately dropped to my knees and gathered up the coins thinking such an action would ease the tension and put Frank and me in Jack's good graces. I scooped up the dimes, nickels, and quarters, stood back up, and held out my hand to Jack.

"Here."

He took the money from my palm, then grabbed hold of my other hand, which was closed shut. I pulled away instinctively, but Jack's grip was too tight.

"What're you doin'?" Frank said. "Let him go."

But Jack didn't let go. He turned my arm so that my hand went palm up, then squeezed harder, forcing my fist to open. It was empty. None of his coins were hiding there.

"Let him go," Frank said louder.

"You shut your mouth."

But Jack did let go. He then turned and paid the cashier, and started for the door.

"Come on." He said over his shoulder as he carried his bag of groceries toward the exit.

Frank hesitated, and I could see he was thinking maybe it would be better to stay here. Call Ma and tell her to meet us in this store. And then I saw him remember we were headed to Yankee Stadium.

We kept walking, Jack up front, Frank and me trailing. We turned off the wide street and cut down a narrower one that was considerably darker. Getting off the large street did bring, if not quiet, a lower volume of ruckus. In fact, the prominent sound we could hear was the Motown hit "I Can't Help Myself." I knew that song quite well, as several months prior it had appeared on my brother's perfect song list no less than four times. Yes, a song can be perfect for more than one activity or occasion. Other notable songs to make numerous appearances on my brother's list were: "Sugar Sugar," "Hot Fun In The City," "Hooked On A Feeling," and the "Theme Song From Hawaii Five-0." But the undisputed king of perfect songs with nine appearances on the perfect song list was "Let It Be" by The Beatles.

But this was not the radio version of "Can't Help Myself," this version was a cappella. And sure enough, midway down the narrow street, leaning in the doorway of a three-story apartment building, were four sharp dressed men singing the song complete with choreography.

"Are they the Four Tops?" Frank asked with a fair amount of excitement brought on by the possibility of seeing the creative force behind a perfect song.

"They're the four morons that keep me up all night," Jack grumbled as we moved past them without a look.

Frank stopped to listen, but I kept following Jack. His big strides hadn't grown shorter since we started out, and I didn't want to lose him when he turned into an alley.

"Frank," I called out.

"Wait a sec."

"We're losin' him."

Frank looked past me and didn't see Jack. This alarmed him and he broke into a run and caught up to me.

"Where'd he go?"

"Down there."

I started into the alley, which was pitch black.

"Wait!"

I stopped.

"Don't go down there."

"You boys comin' or not?" Jack bellowed from the darkness. "Cause I ain't waiting down here in the trash."

Frank kept hold of my jacket and looked into the alley. We could catch glimpses of Jack's eyes and the wedding ring he wore on his left hand.

"Why do we have to go down there?" Frank asked.

"Cause this is how I get to where I live."

"Where's that?"

We heard a clang and caught sight of a fire escape ladder as it slid down to the pavement.

"Up there."

Our eyes moved up the building to the apartments located on the second and third floors.

"You live up there?"

"Something wrong with that?"

"No, 'cept most people use the stairs to go up-stairs."

"Yeah, well, the inside stairwell got water rot on account the landlord, who don't live here, don't fix nothin'. So most people, if they were to take the inside stairs, would go crashin' through the steps into the basement and break their neck on the cement floor. So I'm gonna go up this a way. But bein' how you know so much about so much, I'll give you your choice of which way you wanna go. You feel free to climb those steps and meet me outside Apartment 202."

"I don't wanna go up rotted stairs," I whispered.

Frank zeroed his sights on the apartment on the second floor.

"Is there anybody up there?"

"Sure as hell hope not."

"Who's makin' all that noise?" Came a voice from beneath a flattened piece of cardboard off to our left. "Who won't shut their damn mouths?"

The cardboard covering was pushed aside from underneath and Frank and I looked into the face of an old woman who was covered with dirt. Before she was able to say another word, we were running to where Jack was standing.

"All right, you first," Jack said to Frank.

Frank grabbed hold of the fire escape ladder and climbed quickly and effortlessly.

"Wait up by the first window."

Frank did and Jack turned to me.

"All right, let's go."

I looked up the metal ladder and couldn't get my hands and feet to move.

"Well, come on."

"He don't like heights," Frank said.

"And I don't like the Red Sox, but there it is. 'Sides, ain't the height you gotta worry about, it's the arrival back on the ground if you fall off to be concerned with. The height don't mean nothin'. Long as you stay on the ladder it's just like you on the ground. So just hold tight, keep lookin' up, and be thinkin' you're on the ground. Now go on."

I'm not exactly sure the logic of what Jack said would stand the test of analytical scrutiny, but standing in that dark alley, it made enough sense to get my limbs working. I grasped the ladder and pulled myself up. I climbed slowly, but I climbed steadily. And Jack was right behind me.

"I can't even tell how high I done climbed at the ballpark. Hell, if I had a penny for every step I climbed I'd own Yankee Stadium instead of be sweeping it. Ain't nothin' to be scared of anyhow. My wife used to say the higher you go, the closer you get to the Lord."

I reached another wrung higher.

"Cause if you fall and die you go to heaven?"

Jack paused a moment.

"Never thought of it like that. I suppose that's it."

I reached the spot where Frank was waiting and Jack swung one of his long legs around me and up onto the small metal balcony the fire escape formed outside his window.

"See, we made it fine as sugar."

He pulled a set of keys from his pocket and slid one into the lock that held the window tight.

"All that stuff yours?"

"Will be after I steal it and bring it to my place."

Frank and I froze. And then I heard something I hadn't heard before. I heard Jack chuckle. Not a laugh mind you, maybe not even a chuckle for that matter, but an escape of air that indicated amusement.

He pushed up the window.

"I'll go in first and put on a light."

Jack leaned forward and slid through the opening. He stretched his long leg over the radiator with the skill of a hurdler. A moment later, the room was lit.

"Come on in."

Frank went first. When I made my way into the apartment, my brother was already looking around in amazement. It was a loft-style unit, one room separated into sections by easels containing water color paintings of various baseball stadiums. There was a bedroom area marked off by Yankee Stadium, a living area set-off by Fenway park, and a kitchenette built into one wall beneath a ball park I didn't recognize. But that's not what had Frank amazed. It was that the place was an absolute mess. Like someone dropped all of Jack's belongings from an airplane and this is how they landed.

"Oh man, doesn't anybody clean your house?" Frank said before his mouth and good sense were able to keep his statement from becoming audible.

"Like who? All our women are cleanin' white folks' houses in Scarsdale."

"Is that were your wife is?" I asked.

"Where my wife is ain't none of your business. This is my house and this is the way I like it so don't be touchin' nothin'."

Jack crossed over to his bed, which had a pile of clothes on it.

"Suppose you have company?" Frank wanted to know.

"I don't like company."

"Not ever?" I asked.

"Not ever."

"Not even once?" Frank said.

"Never."

"Don't you get scared bein' alone?" I said.

Jack took a long look at me, then grabbed a NY Yankee's duffle bag from the closet.

"I don't get scared. And I like bein' alone. Don't have to answer a bunch of dumb questions when you're alone."

I could tell Jack was getting annoyed so I stopped asking dumb questions and let him roll a cigarette in peace. But Frank spotted a framed collection of autographed photos of the Yankee greats dating back to DiMaggio and Berra. He studied the photos closely and suddenly realized the young black man posing with the greats, the guy wearing a strange-looking uniform, looked like Jack, only younger.

"That ain't you is it?" Frank asked.

"That was me, ain't me no more."

Jack licked the seam of his hand-rolled smoke and lit up.

"You know all these guys?"

"Standin' with 'em, ain't I?"

"You're bullshi..." Frank uttered.

"Hey! You watch your mouth in my house or the whoopin' Dizzy put on your ass'll seem like moonlight and magnolias."

Frank turned away as Jack shoved some clothes in the duffle bag.

"You ever go on the field at Yankee Stadium?" I asked.

"Every day for the last twenty-seven years."

"Yeah, to rake it," Frank said.

If looks could kill, my brother would've been dead where he stood. As it was Jack's glare stopped him like his feet were nailed to the floorboards. Jack held it a moment, then turned back to his duffle.

"Played an exhibition game against DiMaggio and Williams at the Stadium, April 13, 1941, and struck 'em out two times a piece."

"You're lyin'," Frank said.

"The hell if I am," Jack growled as he stuffed a faded Yankee-towel inside the duffle.

I looked at the photos, at Jack as a young man, towering over the greats.

"What team is that uniform for?"

"Bacharach Giants outta Philadelphia."

"Ha! Ain't no such team," Frank scoffed.

"Well, then you don't know as much as you think you do. Bacharach Giants near won the Negro League title in '36."

"What's a Negro League?" I asked.

"Sure ain't the Major League," Frank answered.

"It was better. Best ballplayers you ever seen. And none of 'em made more'n a penny from it. Take the worst nine of 'em against any team playin' today and that's a goddamn fact. Damn shame nobody ever gonna know it. But there it is."

Jack stamped out his cigarette.

"This your son?"

I was standing next to a shelf made of old two-by-sixes Jack had rigged into the wall. On it, among other knicks and knacks, I saw a photo of a younger Jack standing with an even younger-looking man dressed in a Yankee uniform.

"Willie. That was his name."

"After Mays?"

"Hell no. I had him long before Willie Mays knew what a baseball was. He named after my father."

"Does he play baseball?"

Jack crossed to the shelf and looked at the photo.

"Did."

Jack took the photo down and used his shirttail to clean dust from the glass.

"Stengel said he was pure hitter. God given. Turn on a fastball quicker'n lightning and slap a curve the other way with power."

"Then how come he ain't playin'?" Frank said.

Jack put the photo back on the shelf.

"Got himself killed in Vietnam. Goin' on two years now."

Jack turned away, but I couldn't help thinking how much that photo reminded me of the photo on my nightstand.

"All for nothin'," Jack mumbled. "Just colored folks dyin' for white folks is all. Same as always."

"My cousin Ritchie ain't colored," I said.

"So what?"

"He died there too. Right before Halloween. And he ain't colored."

Music suddenly filled the room and Jack's eyes shot over to Frank, who had opened the top of a small blue and gold music box.

"Get away from that!" Jack barked.

"I didn't do nothin'."

Jack abruptly shut the box, ending the tune.

"Don't be touchin' people's things unless they invite you to! Ain't that what I told ya? That's why I don't want no company. I don't bother with no one and I don't want no one botherin' with me."

"I didn't know . . ."

"You don't know nothin'! Just a little smart ass white boy thinks he can do whatever he please with a colored man's things! 'Cause a colored man don't count! Less than human, so what's it matter!"

Frank was petrified and it showed in the tears welling in his eyes. Jack's body was heaving as he roared. The mere force of it scared Frank to death. I felt the same, but Jack's tirade was aimed at Frank so it hit him with all its force. I only felt the aftershocks.

A silence fell between us. Frank and I huddled off to one side and Jack with the music box on the other. It took a minute, a full minute, but Jack came to feel he'd gone too far with Frank. Bit down more than Frank deserved. So he put down the music box, opened up the drawer in the cabinet, and retrieved two antique baseball cards.

"Here."

Jack held them out, one to each of us.

"Go on. Got autographs on 'em."

I took both cards, then handed one to Frank. I never said thank you, but I nodded and Jack nodded back.

"Well, come on." He said in a hushed tone. "We gotta stop somewheres and then we got a train to catch."

Chapter Eight

My parents met on the last day of August in 1958. My mother, twenty-three at the time but still living at home, decided to take a Saturday off from the chores still assigned her to visit Jones Beach with her cousins, Anna and Virginia. In the dead of winter, at three in morning, without a car on the road, the drive from Pelham Parkway to Jones Beach would take no more than forty-five minutes. However, on a feverishly hot Saturday in the waning days of summer you could be assured of spending two hours in your vehicle before mercifully placing it in park. Still, Jones Beach offered something other public beaches did not possess: a vibrant boardwalk, a restaurant popular with the young, and a large fresh-water pool to compliment the saltiness of the Atlantic Ocean.

The pool is where Anna and Virginia spent the day avoiding sea creatures and hunting young men with chiseled bodies to put to good use at the dance later in the evening. But for my mother, who loved the ocean, the pool served solely to occupy a portion of the crowd. Drawing them off the beach and providing her the necessary space in which to breathe and think. She loved sitting at the edge of the surf, allowing the cool water to caress her feet as she watched the endless arrival of waves from faraway places. And while I cannot know what thoughts filled her mind as she sat staring into the ocean, if she pondered what manner of journey her life would take, or when this odyssey might begin in earnest, I do know she was soothed by the continuous rhythm of the tide. She enjoyed being alone with her thoughts. I favor her in this way. I favor her in most ways.

She loved my father from the start. From before the start. From the moment he placed his blue and white towel on the sand. Before he even said hello. It seems impossible such feelings could occur so quickly, with such depth and power, but then, my father was the tree from which Frank grew. Both possessed an inner light and outer energy that captured the hearts of those around them.

For this I was jealous of Frank. Not for the trait itself, but for the crime of being more like our father. I suspected because of this my mother loved my brother more. How could she not? She had no defenses against my father's love; would she not also be defenseless against Frank's? I know I was.

At the time of their first kiss my father had been a police officer for eight years. They spoke of it only in passing that day at the beach, and my mother was too taken with the handsome stranger to listen to the quiet whispers of concern spoken by her guardian angel. I've often wondered if it would have mattered. If she would have heeded that voice were she not so blinded by love. If she would have considered the life of a policeman's wife and chosen another path. Or perhaps there is such a thing as destiny. Perhaps this was the journey lying in wait as she dipped her toes in the edge of the ocean. If so, the deep and profound happiness my father's love brought into her life came at a price.

My mother and I are worriers. We do not possess the singleness of purpose that blocks the clutter and clang of doubt. We allow all manner of thought, however far-reaching, to enter our minds and this abundance of information is the food on which worry feasts. Whether we were born this way or it came to be, I am not certain. It's possible before meeting my father, my mother did not sleep through the night, that she already feared the knock on the door, the unexpected ring of the telephone, the arrival of a letter with her address typed instead of hand-written, it's possible all those were truths before she met him. I only know they were truths after.

On the morning my father was killed, my mother woke before the sun. Frank had been feverish the night before, and she was concerned his temperature had risen. She was correct. Frank was cooking at a hundred and two degrees and was without question in the grasp of a winter flu. However, Frank was not one to sit still. He didn't sit still for the mumps or the measles; why would he sit still for something as pedestrian as the flu? But my mother worried about pneumonia. She wanted him to rest, and she knew if there were people around, if the possibility of fun existed, however remote, Frank would be on the move. For this reason, she insisted my father take me for breakfast that morning. He didn't want to go. He'd worked eleven days straight and wanted to relax. He wanted to cook up his own eggs and bacon. Watch football. Tinker with the model airplanes he enjoyed crafting. Fall asleep in his favorite chair with the paper across his lap.

But my mother wanted us out. She wanted the house quiet for at least five hours so Frank would sleep. That was her bargain, five hours. My father protested, but, in the end, my mother put her foot down and she never saw him again. Not alive. That's what she lives with. It's what she eats with her food, drinks with her water, it's what she lies next to when she goes to sleep, and what stares into her face each morning when she opens her eyes.

Some fears dissipate when the object of the fear is removed. The fear of darkness subsides with the arrival of light. The fear of height dwindles with a return to earth. But the fear of loss never diminishes. There is no change in circumstance that can remove the object of the fear. It can only be realized. So long as the person you fear losing remains, so does the fear, and when the person is lost, it has been proven right. And then it grows hotter. Burns deeper. It roots itself in your soul and transfers its focus on someone new. In my mother's case, the someone new was her children.

It was that fear which swam through her brain as she ran to the Cutlass. She knew we were alive. But who was this man? This black man? What'd he want? Was Pat right? Had she made a mistake? Supposing something happens? Supposing my boys are hurt, or killed? Reasonable or not, all these questions swirled through her mind, slamming into the sides of her skull as she put the car in gear and stepped on the gas. And they were still coursing through her brain when the car jumped the ragged curb which cut a deep gash in the tire. The air rushed from her wheel as she frantically backed into the street, where the crunch of rim to pavement told her she would not be moving. Not be racing to save her children. Not yet.

We exited Jack's place the same way we entered, down the fire escape. And I was surprised upon my arrival into the alley that I had not even considered the issue of height when I crawled out the window. I was focused on the autographed Yogi Berra rookie baseball card now in my back pocket. Hand under hand I made my way down the iron ladder and all the time I was thinking my father's favorite player had been Yogi Berra. He would have loved to have seen this card. I think he would have framed it and placed it on his work-bench. He would have tried to sneak it into the living room, perhaps a quiet spot on the breakfront, but my mother would have spotted it eventually and send Yogi to the work-bench for sure. Still, my father would have loved to have seen this card.

As I stood in the alley waiting for Frank to climb down, I realized that focus, pinpoint focus, is a powerful tool. It had the ability to shut off the noise in your brain. Make it quiet, which was necessary for calm. Aim your focus somewhere with force and commitment and all other considerations fade into the far reaches of your mind. That's a powerful tool indeed. One whose use I suspect had been mastered by the brave.

"Who'd you get?" Frank asked the second he jumped down from the ladder.

Frank was nothing if not resilient, and the effects of the tongue lashing he got from Jack were erased by whatever was in his back pocket, or mine for that matter.

"Tell you what, don't tell me," Frank said as we waited for Jack. "You don't tell me who you got, I won't tell you who I got. Maybe I got the better one, maybe you do, we won't know. But we'll trade outright. Let the chips fall where they may. What do you say?"

"I got a Yogi Berra rookie card and I ain't tradin'."

"You suck," Frank said.

He glared at me with eyes that shouted he was holding a dud. It was the same look he had on his face the afternoon my father took us to Bat Day at Yankee Stadium. I was handed a Joe Pepitone Louisville Slugger. Joe Pep, besides being a neighborhood favorite, was a first rate hitter. Frank, on the other hand, picked up a Don Nottebart. And while I'm sure Mr. Nottebart was a fine person, he was a second tier pitcher and couldn't hit worth a damn. I voided that proposed trade as well.

"Step aside," Jack hollered, clearing us from his path as he jumped the last three feet.

He then pushed the ladder up to its perch and wiped the dirt from his hand with a green handkerchief he pulled from his pocket.

"You horse tradin' down here?"

"Horses? We ain't got no horses," Frank said.

"I don't mean . . . it's just a way . . . oh the hell with it. Let's get movin'. And stay close. Don't think I didn't see you laggin' back so far as to get yourselves lost."

With that Jack took three giant strides and was nearly at the street. As much as Jack's temper made me nervous, as much as I expected him to erupt at any moment, I felt safer when we were alone with him. On the street, with strangers all around, I found my hands balled and my jaw clenched. I tried to direct my focus onto Yogi

Berra, but I couldn't. What focus I could manage was on the people. The men and the women who kept staring and calling to us as we hurried to keep pace with Jack.

"Don't you wanna know who I got?" Frank said.

"Who did you get?"

"I ain't tellin'. You gotta trade to find out."

"I said I ain't tradin'."

"Then you ain't gonna know."

"Just tell."

"Nope."

"Come on."

"Where we goin'?"

"Fine. I don't care."

"Yes, you do."

"Do not."

"Do too."

"Not."

"Too."

"N."

"T."

"Shut your damn mouths." Jack bellowed. "Givin' me a . . . Holy Mary Mother of Christmas."

Jack stopped short and I watched his head turn and take a long, slow, deliberate look as a young black woman glided past us leaving the scent of fresh flowers in her wake. She seemed the same age as my cousin Debra, which was a little over twenty. But that's where the similarity ended. This woman wore a skin-tight blue dress that stretched over curves that defied gravity. Her skin looked like dark silk and her face was black glass, perfectly sculptured with eyes like two bright shining stars.

Taking our cue from Jack, Frank and I stopped as well, allowing ourselves a good, healthy look at the young woman as she walked away. And the view of her departure, if not better than the view of her arrival, was every bit as awe-inspiring.

"That body could make a bishop kick out a stained glass window," Jack said to nobody in particular. "I gotta remember to send her a thank you card."

"You know her?" I asked.

"I just know bald-headed men and short, fat women. Somethin' like that is harder to come by."

"How come?" Frank wanted to know.

"Cause knowin' a woman gets more difficult with three things. The beauty in her face, the fullness of her breasts, and the slimness of your wallet."

The three of us watched her as she disappeared around a corner.

"And that was just three for three. Come on, let's get 'cross the street to that stand over yonder."

Jack waited for a break in the traffic, then hustled us across the narrow road to a fruit and vegetable stand set up outside a one-room market. Jack gave a quick nod to a bald-headed man of fifty who struggled to lift his short round body from a stool he had positioned near the door.

"See what I mean," Jack said before sending out his hand to shake with the bald fruit peddler. "Coffee."

"Where it at, Jackaroo?"

"Outta my reach."

"Ain't it the truth."

"Hell, I couldn't reach it with a ladder."

"But I still be climbin'."

"All you can do."

Jack took a look at Frank and me.

"How old you two?"

"I'm nine, he's seven," Frank answered.

"You ain't nine," I said.

"I will be in two months."

"But you ain't nine now."

"I'm roundin' up. You round up after the halfway point."

"Still don't make you nine," I said.

"Why don't you shut up."

"Why don't both of you shut up," Jack barked.

We did. Jack handed the shopkeeper a dollar bill.

"Make it nine, seven . . . how many months you say it was to your birthday?"

"Two," Frank offered.

"Nine, seven, two," Jack said to the bald man.

"You got it. So who's them?"

"That's my headache walkin' beside me."

"We're not allowed to drink coffee," I said.

"I can have coffee," Frank countered.

"No, you can't."

"Ma lets me drink coffee when you're not around."

"Does not."

"Who said anything about drinkin' coffee? There ain't no coffee here. I swear you two got voices in your heads and I don't know where in god's good name they're comin' from."

"You asked him for coffee," Frank said.

"I'm Coffee," the shopkeeper said. "That's what peoples call me. Coffee. On account I'm sweet and delicious."

"They call you Coffee 'cause you darker than the bottom of a well at midnight."

"That's what I said, I'm rich, dark, and delicious." Coffee started to laugh.

"So what you got these white boys for? Money or dumb luck?"

"I don't know what the hell I got 'em for yet," Jack said. "Take it slow."

"Only way I can take it."

We moved on from Coffee and the fruit stand but something was gnawing at me.

"He didn't give you nothin'," I said.

"What?"

"Your dollar. He didn't give you nothin'."

"Yeah, you forgot to get somethin' from him," Frank added.

"I got the number," Jack said as he continued walking.

"Where is it?"

"Up here, in my head."

"You gotta pay to get a number?" Frank asked.

"Everybody gotta pay to get a number. Ain't nothin' in life for free. You got any money?"

"No," Frank said.

"Then you don't get no number."

"I got a number in my head right now," Frank countered.

"Ain't the same."

"How so?" I asked.

"It's got to be a special number, a number you got to pay for if you want to play."

"Oh, I get it," Frank turned to me. "Coffee's like Paul Balzano."

"Who?" Jack asked.

"He makes you pay a quarter to take a pee."

"What do you get to play?" I said.

"The number. And if you pick the right one, you win money."

"How much money?"

"Lots of it."

I started to think about this number game. This chance to win lots of money.

"Enough to keep a house in the city?" I asked.

"And then some."

We kept moving. Jack walking with Frank and me quick stepping to keep up.

"How do you know which number to pick?" I said.

"You don't. You gotta have the luck."

"You got the luck?" Frank asked.

"Yep," Jack answered. "But all bad."

I didn't think I was lucky. There was no evidence of it in my life. But it was a chance. And one I thought I should take. I reached deep into my front pocket and I pulled out the silver dollar. The silver dollar my father said would bring me luck. I held it tight in my hand, thought on it a moment, then called out to Jack.

"I want a number."

Jack glanced at me with half a smile, then stopped short when he saw the coin.

"You got a goddamn silver dollar piece in your pocket and you're stealin' a man's hard-earned money outta his business? Not to mention takin' money from me? What the hell's wrong with you?"

"I couldn't use it."

"Why the hell not?"

"It was a present."

"So what?"

"So I couldn't use it. But it brings luck, I think, so I want to get a number and keep my house."

I held the coin out to Jack when I felt someone bump into me from behind. Not on purpose, just an accident, but still the force sent the coin flying from my hand. I watched it hit the sidewalk and begin rolling like a wheel.

"No!" I shrieked as I took off after it.

I weaved in and out of the crowd, working my way closer, keeping my eyes on the coin as I fought through the dozens of legs blocking my way.

"Mickey!" I heard Frank yell.

"Get back here!" Jack demanded.

But I kept moving. I began shoving people, urging them out of my way. They yelled, some shoved back, but I continued to chase my coin. I wasn't giving up. It was too important.

I followed it as it rolled around a corner and angled toward the curb and a heating grate in the sidewalk.

I made a final push and dove for it. Arms outstretched, I sailed through the air, reaching as far as I could as the coin rolled along a thin piece of cross-bar leading to the center of the grate. But instead of grasping the coin, my finger grazed the edge, knocking it from its perch and down through the opening.

"NO!"

Jack and Frank turn the corner as I used all my strength to pull the grate open.

"Wait!" Jack shouted.

I began climbing down the hole with blind determination.

"Get the hell outta there, goddamnit!" Jack yelled.

"Mickey?" Frank shouted.

I was gone, down the ladder that led to total darkness. The only fear I had was the fear of losing my coin. I was of single purpose. I had to find my father's silver dollar.

Up top, Frank stepped toward the ladder but Jack grabbed hold of his shirt and pulled him back.

"Get away from there."

"But he's down there."

Jack looked down the dark, vertical tunnel. "Mickey? You hear me?"

Jack and Frank stood motionless, waiting. And finally they heard me.

"I can't see it!"

I was in a place of muck and mire. Dark and damp. I felt wetness as I used my hands to comb the dirty ground beneath me.

"Get your ass up here now!"

"I gotta find it," I yelled back.

"I'll get you a goddamn number, now get up here or I'll put a whippin' on your ass that you won't soon forget."

It didn't matter what he said. There were no magic words that were going to make me abandon my search.

"Mickey?" Jack cried out again.

"He won't come up without it," Frank said.

"I ain't goin' down there!" Jack howled into the darkness. "You hear me. I ain't goin' down there. So you get up here before you get yourself killed . . . Mickey?"

"We can't leave him in there alone."

Frank's voice shook as he spoke.

"I ain't goin' down there. He gets himself killed, it ain't my fault, no sir."

"Then I'll get him," Frank said.

He tried to push past Jack and drop into the hole. Jack held him back.

"He's down there!" Frank shouted.

Jack held still a moment.

"Goddamnit," Jack roared. "You stay here and don't you let no one close this grate on my head. You hear me?"

"I won't."

Jack stepped into the opening and began climbing down the ladder.

"Brand new shoes," he grumbled. "Your ass better hope there ain't no nonsense down there to step in."

I kept searching for my needle in a haystack as Jack descended the fifteen steps to the bottom of the dark tube.

"Mickey?"

"Over here."

The downward chute from the sidewalk led to a long tunnel dimly lit by wall lanterns. Jack caught sight of my silhouette. He lit a match, which put me in full view.

"You know where you at? Now go back up that ladder."

"I gotta find it."

"They got bats and rats big as airplanes down here, and who knows what else is slitherin' around all this muck."

"My dad gave it to me."

"You'll get another one."

"No. I gotta find that one."

Jack grabbed hold of me and was about to pull me to the ladder.

"Please!" I cried out.

He looked into my eyes. I'm not sure exactly what he saw. But he let go of my arm.

"Five minutes. Five minutes and we're leavin'."

I stepped back and continued to search as Jack knelt down with the match to shine some light.

"Don't know what you think you're gonna find down here in all this crap."

But he kept looking. Through the garbage, through the mud, through the poop. Then his match reflected off something metal. He brought the flame closer. What he saw was not the coin, but subway tracks. And from the darkness, we heard the clang and screech of an approaching train.

"Oh hell."

The match burned the tip of Jack's finger forcing him to drop it into the muck returning the tunnel to darkness.

"Get up there now!" Jack boomed over the approaching roar of the train. "Right now!"

"I gotta find it."

"I don't give a good goddamn!" Jack screamed.

He lit another match. "You get up there!"

"No."

I wasn't quitting. Not for him, not for the train, not for anything. I was getting that coin. I fell to my hands and knees, scouring as much area as I could. All the while the train was charging closer and closer.

"Goddamnit!"

Jack grabbed hold of me and lifted me in the air. I fought against his grip, but it was too strong to break.

"NO!"

"I got it." Jack said.

"Let me see it!"

My voice was drowned by the train and both of us could feel the tracks vibrating under its force.

"I said I got it, now get up there."

"I don't believe you!"

The headlight of the lead car turned the bend and caught us in its grip.

"GO!"

Jack flung me onto the ladder. I gripped it with both hands.

"GO!"

I started to climb as light from the train reached up the vertical shaft toward the street.

"Hurry!" Jack urged.

He stood at the bottom of the chute with the train less than twenty yards away.

He then pushed me up, grabbed hold of the ladder, and curled his legs in tight as the train stormed through.

I reached the sidewalk and Frank pulled me up. We heard Jack scream, but only for an instant as all sound was swallowed by the roar of the rushing train. As it barreled through the tunnel it shot light up the chute, flashing over Frank and me like a strobe. Car after car.

Seemingly endless. The biting tone of steel on steel ripping our ears until we had to cover them to stop the pain.

And then it was gone. All that was left was the whoosh of warm air pushing up from deep within the earth. Frank and I looked down into the darkness.

"I don't see him," Frank said.

We kept watching. And slowly, we saw the top of Jack's head as he climbed the ladder.

"We thought you were dead," Frank said.

"So did I." Jack exhaled.

With fear still frozen on his face, Jack pulled himself from the hole and closed the grate.

"Where's my dollar?"

Jack shot around and stared a hole in my face.

"Where's my dollar? That what you wanna say to me? I nearly got killed cause a that damn coin."

"You didn't get it. You're a liar! I knew you didn't get it! I knew it!"

I reached for the grate and started to push it open. Jack stomped it with his foot and slammed it shut.

"How would you feel if I got smashed to pieces down there on account of one dollar? Huh? Or maybe a colored man don't mean as much to you as a coin."

"My dad gave it to me."

Jack kept staring at me. He held out his fist. Slowly, he unclenched his fingers. Resting safely against his skin was the silver dollar.

"Go on, it's what you wanted so bad."

I took the coin, cleaned off the mud with my thumbs, and buried it deep in my pocket.

"Next time a train is comin' and I say move your ass, you move your damn ass."

Jack turned and strode back toward the corner.

"Come on." Frank said.

And the two of us hustled after him.

When the phone rang, my mom considered not answering.

Sal, from the gas station on the corner of Waring and Eastchester, had been kind enough to make a house call and was just finishing up with the spare tire. She hurried toward the door, keys in her hand, but then stopped as the phone continued to ring. Whoever this was didn't give up after four rings. What if it was Frank or Mickey? What if something happened to them? What if plans had changed? My mother reached the front door and called to Sal.

"Sal?"

He looked up from the car as he tightened the last of the lug nuts.

"I'll be right there."

He waved and my mother turned back and answered the phone.

"Hello?"

"Good, you're still there."

It was my Uncle Pat.

"I'm just over the water in Jersey. I want you to wait. I should be at your place in half an hour."

"No, that's too long, I've got to leave now."

Waiting meant standing still. And standing still was the hardest thing my mother could do at that moment. The more still her body, the more restless her mind. In the time it took to contact Sal and get him to the house to fix the tire, she conjured all sorts of scenarios in her head. And all of them ended with Frank and me dead.

"Just wait for me. Thirty minutes."

"I'm going for my kids."

"Carol..."

"I'm leaving, Pat. I'll talk to you later."

My mom was ready to hang up. She had pulled the phone from her ear. But then she heard the words.

"The guy's got a sheet."

The information hit her like a sledge-hammer. It woke all the thoughts she'd been trying to push to the far reaches of her mind where unspeakable fears live and breathe.

"How do you know?"

"I called Kevin's old partner at the station. They ran a check on this Jack Hutchins."

"What'd they say?"

"About six weeks ago he couldn't get his wife into the emergency room at City General because she was colored. She had a heart attack or something where she was workin'. Cleanin' or something. Anyway, by the time he got her uptown she was dead. He went nuts. Beat living hell out of the two ambulance guys, put one in the hospital and the whole time swearing he was gonna go back to City General and kill somebody."

"Oh my god."

My mother now took responsibility. She had allowed us to be in this man's care. Whatever happened to her children would be her fault.

"They locked him up for a week, but you know how that is. They got a civil suit going, the ambulance guys, but the criminal charges didn't go nowhere. So just wait for me. I'll be there in thirty minutes."

"Hurry."

"I'm on my way."

Uncle Pat hung up. My mother did the same. Then she slowly slumped into the chair she had inherited from her Aunt Nettie. Slumped with the weight of the guilt that began with sending my father out to breakfast on that Sunday in December. The guilt that grew with every silence that filled our house since. That put us in the hands of a man who threatened to kill those responsible for the death of his wife.

"Mrs. O'Neil?"

My mother looked up and saw Sal standing just outside the screen door.

"Everything OK?"

Chapter *Nine*

We followed Jack to the entrance of a rundown four-story apartment building on a side street about a mile and half from his home. It'd been a long, silent walk to get there, and Jack's step was not quite as quick as earlier in the evening. He was still shaken from the episode with the subway train and I could sense he had kept hold of the animosity he felt toward me. At several points since we emerged from the tunnel I heard Jack mumble to himself. I couldn't completely make out the words, but I knew the intention. I valued a coin more than his life. More than a black man's life. It wasn't true. But he believed it, and that wasn't good.

"Where're you goin'?" Frank asked as Jack reached for the door-knob.

"First of all, I'm seriously considering dumpin' the two of you right here and now before I get killed for sure."

"We're not goin' up there."

"And second, you are children! You can tell you're children 'cause you're heard when you should only be seen. I'm a man, close to sixty-five years old. And where I go is for me to decide and you to follow."

126

Jack took hold of the door-knob with one of his enormous hands and swung it open so hard I thought it would fly off the hinges.

"Now move your asses."

"We don't want to go up there," Frank pressed.

"Neither do I. But there it is."

The Mexican standoff lasted all of five seconds before I started to step forward. I was still scared of Jack, and I know my mother and Uncle Pat would raise holy hell if they saw me walking into this apartment building with a man I didn't know, but I was beginning to think that I did know him. Maybe not by words, but by deeds. It was just a feeling I had. One hard to understand or throw your arms around, but a feeling to be paid attention to nonetheless. Perhaps that's why I was willing to follow him inside. Because I did know him. Or maybe I was just more scared of what lived out on these streets. What we'd been walking past for better than forty minutes. Either way, I stepped forward ready to follow Jack, when Frank grabbed hold of me and pulled me back.

"We ain't goin' in there."

"Then don't."

Jack disappeared inside the building and slammed the door behind him. I could hear the echo of his footsteps as he climbed to the second floor, then the third. But at that point they stopped, which left a lot of space to hear the other sounds that surrounded us. We heard music. Drum rhythms, fast and percussive, pulsing from windows overlooking the street. We heard yelling and screaming. Not cries for help, but with the inflection of scolding, both child and mate. We heard car engines roar. Sirens blare. Firecrackers exploding, which, if not for experience, I would have thought were gunshots. All these noises. Familiar noises, but here, in this place, they became the voice of danger.

"Let's go in," I urged.

"You don't know what's in there."

"You don't know what's *out here*."

"But we can run out here. They can hold you prisoner in there. And then they cut off your finger and mail it to your parents and ask for money."

"Do not."

"Do so. Uncle Pat told me. And we ain't got no money, so they're just gonna keep cuttin' off our fingers till we ain't got no more. Then they're gonna start on our toes."

"So what are we . . ."

". . . gonna do?" Frank said, finishing the sentence for me. "We're gonna wait here till he comes out. If he comes out."

"You think they're gonna cut off his fingers?"

"Maybe, who knows."

A moment went by and I asked Frank what had been on my mind all day.

"You think we're gonna have to live with him?

"I don't know. Maybe."

"You think he wants Ma?"

"I don't know, quit askin' me so much stuff."

I was able to hold my tongue another eight seconds.

"What do you think Uncle Pat's gonna do when we get back? You think we're gonna get hit?"

"Hell yeah, we're gonna get hit."

"You think we're gonna get hit?!"

"Yeah."

"But you said they'd crap the floor. Crap the floor and be so glad nothin' happened to us we wouldn't have to move to Uncle Pat's."

"But I never said we wouldn't get hit too."

"Why didn't you say that part?!"

"Cause you would have chickened out. Now shut up for two minutes and sixteen seconds."

We stood quietly in front of the building. We didn't turn our eyes in the same direction, but we saw the same things. People. People staring at us. From in front of other apartment buildings. From opened windows. From passing cars.

Then something hit Frank in the side of the face, just under his right eye.

"What the hell?" Frank said.

On the ground we saw a bottle cap with its edges flattened like a Frisbee. I looked at Frank's cheek and saw a tiny droplet of blood slipping from a narrow, paper-thin cut where the cap hit.

"Must be rainin' Coca-Cola."

We heard laughter, which drew our eyes toward seven boys across the street. They were all about ten or twelve, all black, all bigger than us, and I had no idea where they came from.

"What you doin' here in my neighborhood, 'cept gettin' rained on?" said the biggest kid in the group, as he snapped his fingers and sent another bottle cup whizzing past Frank's face.

I deduced he was the leader. It usually goes that way: the biggest kid, the kid who can beat hell out of everyone else leads and does most of the talking.

We didn't answer. Neither the question nor the bottle cap. But we kept our eyes fixed on the group as they stepped off the sidewalk into the street. That's when I saw him. Lying back toward the rear of the group was Nelson, the black Ojibwa. But neither Frank nor I expected his allegiance to fall with his fellow Indians.

"I asked you a question, dumb ass. What're you doin' in my neighborhood? I didn't invite you."

He lit a cigarette and tossed the match into the street.

"Any of you invite two white boys to my neighborhood?"

He looked at his friends, who assured him they sent no invitations.

"Maybe these white boys is just retarded."

Frank and I took a step back, closer to the apartment building, when the leader led his gang toward us. They crossed the street slowly, aware that the longer it took, the more frightened we became. And they were enjoying it.

"That it? You two retarded? Maybe your mama and papa are brother and sister or somethin' like that?"

They stepped up the curb and walked us farther back until we were pressed against the door.

"Yeah, that must be it, their mama and daddy are brother and sister. Now let me hear you say it. My mama and daddy are brother and sister and I'm just a retarded white boy."

He set his dark gaze upon us. First me, then Frank. Shifting it back and forth like he was reciting eenie-meenie-minee-moe in his head.

"I said, say it."

He flicked his cigarette into Frank's face as the door behind us flew open.

"Get outta here!"

Frank and I turned to see an old woman of seventy with a broom she carried like a baseball bat. She was big. Not as big as Jack, but big for a woman, and she looked like Jack. She had the same broad mouth, and the shape of their wide-set eyes were identical ovals.

"Get your asses home right now," she hollered.

"You don't own the street," the leader retaliated.

"But I'm gonna own your ass if I get off this stoop." And with that she drove the tip of the broom handle into his chest and pushed him back with a heavy lunge.

"Now git."

I could see the Leader was in a bit of pain from that broom shot, but he wasn't about to show it in front of his gang. So he began to shadow box like he was Muhammad Ali.

"Come on, Grace, I'm ready for you." He said, showing off his boxing skill.

"Don't you try me, boy. Two days from now when you wake up in the hospital you gonna wish you didn't try me."

"I'm gonna knock you out, Grace."

With that, Grace pushed forward with her broom handle and the boys scattered and ran laughing across the street.

"That's right." Grace called after them. "You go on home before I call your mama and tell her I had to beat the black off your ass."

The boys kept laughing and running as Grace turned her gaze upon Frank and me.

"You Mickey?"

Before I could open my mouth Frank said, "Maybe."

"You must be Frank." Grace said. "Well, never you mind those boys, they just ain't used to white folks bein' here is all. They're good boys really."

"They're jerks," Frank said, still stinging from the bruise to his pride which comes with a bottle cap and cigarette flicked in your face.

"Let he who hath no sin cast the first stone," Grace countered.

"What?" I asked.

"It's from the Bible. Means don't be throwin' rocks if you live in a glass house. Jack's lookin' in on our pa. It's gonna be a few, so maybe you boys should come on up. I got some lemonade."

Frank didn't budge.

"You don't like colored folk much do you, Frank?"

"They don't like me neither."

"Lord if you don't sound like Jack."

Grace pushed the door open wide enough for her to fit through.

"Well, if you wanna come in it's number 4C."

She stepped inside and once again I could hear footsteps climbing up the stairwell to the fourth floor.

"Let's go in."

"No."

"She ain't gonna cut off our fingers, she was talkin' Bible talk."

"Ma said don't go in nowhere."

"We already been in Jack's apartment."

"I know, cause I forgot. But I remember now and she said don't go in nowhere."

Suddenly another bottle cap hit Frank in the chest. We heard the laughter and looked up to see that group of kids back where they started.

"You still ain't said it yet?" The Leader scoffed as he started across the street.

I didn't need any more motivation than that. Before that kid planted his foot down one more time I was through the door and running up the stairs. I reached the fourth floor in fifteen seconds and cut down the dark hallway until I reached apartment 4C.

I looked back down the hall and saw Frank comin' like his back was on fire.

"Don't you knock," he hollered.

I knocked. Almost immediately the door opened and I was looking into the face of a six-year-old girl in a white dress with a blue ribbon tied around her braided hair.

"Well, what do you want?" She said like she was fifty years old.

Frank reached the door and stumbled to a stop when he saw the girl.

"You shouldn't run in the hall, it disturbs the neighbors."

The three of us stood in silence.

"Well, what do you want?" She asked again.

"The lady said we could have lemonade?" I said.

"What's twelve times thirteen?" She asked with a schoolteacher's staccato.

"Huh?" Frank answered.

"Twelve times thirteen, that's the password."

"Just open the door," Frank said asserting his superiority by virtue of age.

"Sorry. You have to answer correctly to get in."

We stared at her, dumbfounded. I think had we known there would be math involved we could've handled twelve times thirteen, but this caught us off guard.

"Ask me to help you and if I decide I like you, then I will."

"Forget it," Frank said.

"That's fine, 'cause I don't like you anyway, so you'd be without help. But I like him just fine."

That was the first time ever. The first time someone actually said they liked me more than Frank. And I know as brothers I shouldn't relish in such sentiments, but I can't deny my chest swelled when she said it.

"So if you ask me..."

"Would you help please?" I said.

"Certainly. Twelve times thirteen is one hundred fifty-six. Because twelve times twelve is one hundred forty-four as everyone knows, and you just add another twelve and you have one hundred fifty-six."

She abruptly closed the door and left us standing in the hall.

"She's nuts," Frank said.

I knocked on the door and it opened once again.

"Yes?" She said.

"One hundred fifty-six."

"You can come in."

I stepped inside and she was about to close the door on Frank's head when I heard him squawk.

"Hey!"

"Password please."

"One hundred fifty-six, now open the damn door."

She opened it wide.

"Welcome to our home."

She shut it behind us and latched the two deadbolts.

The apartment was tiny. Smaller than Jack's, but neat as a pin. As dirty as the building and the hallway were on the outside, that's how clean it was on the inside. The one strange thing I did notice was the furnishings. They were all mismatched. The couch was different from the chair, which was different from the other chair and so on. As if all these items were purchased at different yard sales and brought together as strangers. But it was the smell that really caught my attention. I'd smelled that smell once before when my grandmother came to die with us. It took six weeks for her to do it and the entire time our house smelled just like this apartment.

"Follow me."

The young girl guided Frank and me into the kitchen, where Grace was pouring lemonades.

"I put two spoons a sugar in for you."

She placed the glasses, which were not real glasses but mason jars, on the small kitchen table and we took our seats. Grace left us the pitcher and sugar bowl in case we wanted seconds.

"Rose," Grace said to the little girl. "You entertain our guests. And you boys enjoy your lemonade. I'm gonna check on Jack, see how he's movin' along."

Her hand rested on my shoulder as she crossed toward the living room. It was only for a second, but in that second, I felt the warmth of her touch. Not simply the temperature, though that was warm as well. I felt her warmth. It was a wondrous thing and not one I've felt many times in my life, even from people who love me. Grace had a gift.

"Bet you don't know who the sixteenth president was?" Rose said before taking a tiny sip from her glass.

"I don't care." Frank responded. "I don't care what twelve times thirteen is and I don't care who the sixteenth president was."

"You just don't know, so it makes you mad."

"I'm not listening to you."

I must admit, as I sat sipping my sweetened lemonade and listening to this six-year-old girl run circles around Frank, I was smiling inside.

"Abraham Lincoln. He was the sixteenth president. He freed the colored people, then got shot at the movies. I bet you didn't know any of that."

"I bet you don't know that your epidermis is showin'," Frank said with smug enthusiasm. "We're staring right at it."

Rose looked at us and took another sip.

"Everybody's epidermis is showing. Unless they stuff you inside a big trash bag. 'Cause it's your skin."

I was awed.

Frank was crushed.

"You can't fool me because I'm a genius. It's true. Everyone says so. My IQ is 197. I could read when I was three and not just *See Spot Run* but the newspaper and books like *Black Beauty*. I've skipped two grades already,

I can play the violin, and I'm going to be president one day."

"Girls can't be president," Frank dismissed as he polished off his first glass of lemonade.

"They will when I grow up."

"Then you ain't as smart as you think you are."

"How many feet are there in a mile?"

"How many baseball players on the field at one time?

"Thirteen," She answered.

"Wrong. Nine."

"Not if the bases are loaded and there's a batter at the plate."

I thought the top of Frank's head was going to blow clean off. But he was outgunned with Rose. Anybody would be. She was six years old and you could already see it in her eyes. Brains. More than brains. Intelligence. Scary, intimidating intelligence. But she also had another quality. Leadership. If you were in a foxhole with a group of people trying to figure out how to get past the enemy, her voice is the one you'd listen to. I had no doubt she would one day be president.

"You stop teasing them," Grace said as she came back into the kitchen and topped off our glasses with the remaining lemonade.

"We're just playing," Rose assured her. "Right Mickey?"

"Yep," I was in love.

"No, we're not," Frank countered. "And what's taking him so long?"

Frank, as cranky as I'd ever seen him, stormed from the table and cut through the living room. But when he reached the entrance to the bedroom, he stopped.

Inside the room he saw Jack carrying a thin, sickly old man from the bathroom.

"Yes sir, Yankees playin' like old women," Jack said as he lowered the old man into the bed.

"I don't think one of 'ems got a hair on his ass longer than a quarter inch."

I stepped up behind Frank and watched quietly as Jack pulled a clean, pale blue sheet up over the man's frail body.

"You watch them Mets over in Queens. They the ones gonna make a run at it."

The old man seemed to move his thin, chapped lips and Jack put his ear close.

"No, Papa," Jack said as he rubbed his hand over the man's head. "Willie don't play no more."

"What is it?" I whispered to Frank.

"His father is crippled or something."

"He's what?"

"Like Pinky's grandpa."

The old man mumbled again and Jack leaned close. I saw his expression change as he listened. He seemed to look older himself.

"His mama's gone too," Jack said, wiping the saliva from his father's lips. "I just let her go."

Jack's eyes began to well up and his breath grew heavier.

"She was lookin' right at me, and I didn't do nothin'. I just let those sons a dogs take her from me. And now she's gone. Everyone is gone."

I felt guilty watching this moment between Jack and his father. I knew it was private, but I couldn't turn myself away and neither could Frank. We continued to watch as Jack kissed the old man.

"I gotta get goin'," Jack said to his father. "You take care of yourself. And don't be askin' Rose to sneak you no sippin' whiskey."

The old man smiled a crooked smile and Jack turned for the door, catching a glimpse of Frank and me as we scrambled back into the living room.

We were crossing toward the kitchen when I spotted a framed photo of Rose in the arms of a black Santa Claus.

"Santa's a Negro?" I blurted in complete shock.

I picked up the photo for a closer inspection.

"I don't believe it. Frank, Santa's a Negro."

Rose strode into the living room and snatched the photo from my hands.

"Of course he is."

"No way." Frank argued. This was a line in the sand that would not be crossed.

"I'm sorry to disappoint you," Rose said as she returned the photo to its proper place. "But he's most certainly colored."

"We've seen him," I said. "At our house. He brought us double-trailer Texaco gas and oil trucks."

"And we seen him at the stores too and he's white," Frank added.

"Those Santas were make-believe, just people hired to pretend. The real Santa is colored. He came in through the window last Christmas 'cause we don't have a chimney and he brought all kinds of presents."

"You're lying," Frank said.

"We got a subway to catch."

Jack stepped from the bedroom directly into the Santa Claus controversy.

"Isn't Santa colored Uncle Jack?"

Jack stopped in his tracks. He was in it all right. He looked at Rose, looked at Frank and me and thought what to say. But he wasn't in a charitable mood. He hadn't been in a charitable mood for some time.

"Yes, he is. Seen him many a time over the years and Santa is as colored as me. In fact, he's darker than me. Black like the bottom of well he is."

"Told you."

I was crushed, so was Frank. Actually, more than crushed. How was this possible?

"He's both."

Grace hurried into the room shooting daggers at Jack with her eyes.

"And more."

"How so?" I asked.

"Santa's magical. He understands that people ain't as understandin' as him. Not so charitable toward people who look different than they do. So he changes himself from color to color. This way when people see him at Christmas it's easier for 'em to digest. So he's colored when he's visitin' colored folks, white when visitin' white folks, Chinese when he's . . ."

"Chinese?!" Frank spit out.

"Grandma, Santa Claus is not Chinese."

Grace rolled her head back and let out a laugh that shook her body from top to bottom, shook the whole apartment. Shook it till we all started to laugh. Even Jack.

Chapter Ten

"That's another sixty cents you owe me," Jack said. He pumped change into the turnstile and hustled us onto the subway platform. Except for the trash it was nearly empty, but in that respect it was the most crowded subway platform I'd ever seen. Bottles, cans, old news-papers, gum wrappers, everything and anything was strewn from one end to the other. The few people we did see seemed to be living there. They had old blankets and coats wrapped around them, and they sipped from bottles concealed in brown paper bags like the bus driver, and they looked out into the dark tunnels without seeing a thing.

Frank wandered toward the ledge and looked down toward the tracks. He saw what he expected to see, steel rails and a plethora of garbage. But there's some-thing about trains and subways that calls to you. They pull you toward them with the power and force that drives them forward. And that pull is never stronger than when you are a child.

"You fall in there, don't expect me to come get ya," Jack reminded him. "My climbin' into tunnels is over and done with. And I'm runnin' late as it is."

"I'm not gonna fall," Frank said.

"Just so you know."

Jack reached deep inside his pocket for his rolling papers and tobacco pouch.

"How come your father can't walk or talk or nothin'?" I asked.

"He got a stroke."

Jack began to roll the paper into a fine tube.

"What's a stroke?"

"It's like a heart attack, but in your brain. Kills you without killin' you."

I watched Jack lick the seam tight, then strike a match.

"Better you just die."

"It's better to die?"

"When livin's worse than dyin', yeah, it's better."

"Wouldn't you miss him?"

"Wouldn't I miss him? What kinda fool question is that? Of course I'd miss him, what the hell kinda person you think I am."

Jack took a draw on his cigarette.

"But sometimes it's better you let go," he said. "Better to move on to another place."

"Supposing they don't want to?" I asked. "Supposing they don't want to move on to another place? . . . What if they weren't supposed to go at all?"

Jack paused. He slowly withdrew his hand-rolled smoke from his mouth. He wasn't looking at me as much as into me. I felt as though he knew I was asking him something that meant something to me. Something personal.

"You got somethin' on your mind?"

I shrugged my shoulders. There was a chance there, a chance to speak and I didn't take it. I didn't have the courage. It was only Jack and me, Frank was at the far end of the platform. I was standing with a man who didn't know my family, didn't know my mother, my Uncle Pat, any of our friends or any of my cousins. Anything I said to him would be between him and me, and still I couldn't do it. Jack waited, then saw whatever I held inside wasn't ready to come out.

"I don't expect anybody ever wants to go," Jack said. "But sometimes it's the best thing."

I hung on his words, hoping there was something he would say that would make sense of things. Give me a reason. Give me an excuse.

"But sometimes it's the worst thing," Jack said. "Cause they young, or it happens sudde . . . or maybe shouldn't have happened at all."

His gaze changed with those last words. He was talking about himself. But I still needed to know more.

"Then won't they be mad?" I asked "Mad at the person who made them go? Whose fault it was?"

Jack considered what I said. Considered how it applied to him, and his wife. Maybe even his son. But mostly he considered how it applied to me. He studied me as he took a long, slow pull on his cigarette. And kept on studying me as he dropped it to the floor and crushed it with his shoe.

"I don't know. Maybe. I've wondered myself from time to time."

"Cause of your wife?" I asked.

"Yeah, 'cause of my wife."

Then he hesitated, took a breath, and said, "You worried somebody mad at you?"

The words hung in the air like dense fog. The truth is like that when it's spoken out loud. It doesn't dissolve like so many things people say to one another. It holds hard and heavy. It wraps its arms around you and won't let you ignore it or pretend it's not there. And at that moment, as I felt my body heat up, and my face and hands tingle, I looked into Jack Hutchins's face and searched my soul for courage. I found a small piece. Enough to nod my head one time.

Jack's head seemed to nod with mine. Like he already knew. And I believe he did. Not exactly what had happened, but that there was a weight on me. One whose effect he was coming to see and feel.

"It's one of those things you can never know for sure I guess." He took a moment to search for words. "I know what the church say."

By the inflection in his voice and the manner in which his eyes looked up as if searching for something, I knew he wasn't just speaking to me. He was speaking to both of us.

"The church say when they get to where they're goin' they know it's right to be there no matter whether they was suppose to go or not, and so they're happy, happy to be with God. And they ain't mad at no one. So maybe that just leaves us to be mad at ourselves."

We stood quietly, side by side. An express train moving south on the far side of the platform burst from the darkness and raced by, drowning all sound with the screech of its wheels. Wheels that spit fire and sparks as they barreled through the tunnel, stirring up the trash and the hot air and the emotions inside me. When it finally disappeared back into the darkness Jack spotted Frank drawing something on the platform floor.

"What you drawin' there?" Jack called out.

"Scully board," Frank answered.

"Scully board?"

Jack crossed toward Frank and saw the numbered squares my brother had drawn with a piece of chalk he stole from Dizzy's Diner.

"You don't know what scully is?" Frank said as he pulled two bottle caps filled with colored wax from his pocket.

"Should I?"

"It's only the best game there is. I'll show ya."

Frank placed the wax-filled bottle caps onto the designated starting line and got down on one knee.

"You gotta flick your scully—the bottle cap is your scully—you gotta flick your scully with your finger and slide it into the next numbered box. But it can't be touchin' the lines, it's gotta be completely inside the box. So we're shootin' for box number one."

Frank flicked his scully and sent it sliding over across the platform floor and into the center of box number 1.

"Then you get to flick it to the next box, and the next, and the next till you get to the last box which is marked home. And the first scullier to get home wins."

"Seems straight forward enough?"

"Mick, you go first," Frank said as he walked down and picked up his scully. "I was just scullyin' to show him so he gets it."

I pulled out my scully, which was a Coca-Cola cap filled with green and white wax, and laid it on the starting line. I cocked my finger, let out a breath nice and slow, and flicked, sending my scully across the floor into the center of box number one and out the other side.

"Too hard," Frank said before turning to Jack. "You go second."

"I don't want to go second," Jack said.

"You want to go last?"

"I don't want to go at all."

"Why not?"

"I ain't interested in scully."

"Afraid you're gonna stink?"

"No."

"It's okay if you stink. You ain't never scullied before. Me and Mick figure you're gonna stink the whole place up so bad we'll have to hold our noses."

"You got a mouth on you that be beggin' for either a slap full of knuckles or a big bar of soap."

Frank turned to me.

"He's scareder than I thought."

They say with boxers the last thing to go is the power. But it isn't. With boxers, and nearly every other man or boy, the last thing to go is pride. Jack got down to one knee, lined up the red-wax scully Frank put there for him, and cocked his finger.

"Can't flick it too hard or too soft."

"Don't be schoolin' me boy. I played marbles before you was a fart in your daddy's ass."

With that, Jack flicked his scully and shot it perfectly into box number one, dead center.

"Made my lunch money playin' marbles against big mouth know-it-alls like you, Frank."

With the calm and cool of Minnesota Fats, Frank placed his scully on the starting line.

"That so?"

He then flicked his finger and sent his scully screaming toward box number one, where it collided with Jack's scully and sent it flying to the end of the platform.

"What the hell was that?" Jack protested.

Frank pointed to his scully sitting alone and dead center in box number one.

"That, Jack, was scully."

Frank started to laugh when Jack suddenly heard something that made his entire body tense up like a piece of petrified wood. It was footsteps. Hard rubber heels on the platform floor. He turned toward the sound sand saw a cop, tall as him and with a nightstick in his hand, moving toward us.

"Damn," Jack said under his breath.

"It's just a cop," Frank said.

"He asks you, you tell 'im I work for your father."

"What for?" Frank asked.

"Never mind what for, you just do it."

"But our father's dead," Frank said.

Jack turned to me, looked right through me, the words we exchanged had meaning to him now, he knew where they came from, but the cop was bearing down on us and there wasn't time to talk or think. Jack got to his feet.

"Just tell him anyways."

Something strange happened when Jack stood up. He was smaller. Not as tall as before. His shoulders, normally back and ramrod straight, were hunched down and he looked up through his eyebrows as his head was tilted toward the floor.

"Evenin'," Jack said as the cop stepped close. "The boys and I . . ."

The cop shot out his night stick and pushed it into Jack's neck and lifted up his chin.

"Did I ask you anything?"

"No," Jack replied.

"No what?" The cop countered, pressing his baton deeper into Jack's throat.

"No, sir."

"Then shut that hole in your face."

Frank and I stood still as trees. We'd seen boys scolded, put in their place and made to feel small and low, but we'd never seen it happen to a man. And it was happening. Jack was even smaller now than when he first stood up. And I knew part of that was because we were there watching.

"Show me some ID," the cop said.

Jack reached into his pocket, but the cop quickly moved his baton from Jack's neck to his hand and pinned it tight.

"Slow."

Jack slowly removed his wallet and handed over his I.D. card, which the cop inspected. We watched him read over the card and waited for what was next.

"What's a nigger doing with two white boys, Jack?"

"I work for their father. In the Bronx. Handyman, mechanic, odd jobs. I was just takin' the boys . . ."

"Shut your mouth," the cop barked.

And Jack did as he was told. Like a child reprimanded by a stern and merciless teacher. I was looking into Jack's down-turned eyes when the cop shifted his focus toward Frank and me.

"I know you boys might be scared of him, but I ain't. So if he's lying to me, I want you to tell me and I'll take care of it."

My eyes turned toward Jack.

"Don't look at him," the cop ordered. "You look at me."

I did as I was told.

"Is he lying to me?"

His eyes were boring into me. Reading my face. Looking for the answer he hoped was true.

"He's . . ." Frank began but the cop quickly cut him off.

"I'm talkin' to him."

The cop pointed to me and stepped a foot closer. He crouched down so that his face was even with mine.

"He's lying to me, isn't he?"

The cop's face was cold and cruel. Not like any of the men my father introduced us to the afternoon he brought us to his station house.

"You can tell me. He won't do nothing."

I looked at the cop and I could smell the sour fumes of alcohol on his tongue.

"He works for my dad."

The cop looked at me a moment longer, then stood up from his crouch and handed Jack his I.D.

"What are they doing in Harlem, Jack?"

"Their folks was workin' today and their pa asked me to watch 'em."

"Did he ask you to bring them to Harlem? Spend the day with a bunch of niggers?"

"I needed to pick up some things from . . ."

"I don't give a damn what you needed."

Jack eyes were on the floor.

"You take these boys outta the Bronx and bring them up here again and so help me god, Jack, I'll cave your head in with this stick. You understand that?"

"Yes."

The cop suddenly whacked Jack across the stomach with his club. Frank and I nearly jumped back, startled by the swiftness and force of the blow which echoed down the platform. We watched as Jack doubled over, clutching his mid-section.

"What'd you say?" the cop said.

"Yes, sir."

A rumble filled the platform, growing louder until a train whooshed out from the dark tunnel and screeched to a halt directly beside us.

"This your train?"

"Yes, Sir."

"Then you get on it. And you remember what I told you."

"Yes, Sir."

Jack turned to Frank and me and spoke softly. "Come on."

He walked behind us as we stepped onto the subway car and took some seats. I kept my eyes on the cop as the train doors closed and we pulled from the station, but Jack kept his on the floor. And they remained there until we were far from the platform. Safely in the cool, dark tunnel ahead. Then his body began to straighten. His shoulders broke upward, his back stiffened, his chest filled, but not with relief, or feelings of self-worth, but with anger, and with hate. His hands were tight, balled fists and his jaw was set tight as he ground tooth to tooth. His eyes stared out across the subway car and his mind was fixated on a single emotion. Hate. I could see it, and I could feel it.

"Why didn't you tell him the truth?" Frank said.

Jack didn't turn to face Frank. He kept his gaze straight ahead, and when he spoke it was low, almost guttural.

"He'd take us in."

"Why?"

"Cause he wouldn't't've believed it."

"Why not?" Frank wanted to know.

"Cause I don't believe it," Jack barked.

He shifted in his seat, but he wouldn't look at us when he spoke. And I saw there was something else besides the anger and hate which kept Jack's eyes forward. It was humiliation. That was at the core of all he was feeling.

"Better he thinks I work for you. He can understand that."

We sat quietly, our bodies jerking back and forth with the movement of the train. Flashing from light to darkness, and back to light.

We remained in our seats through our first stop, barely watching as other black people exited and entered the car. And then we were moving again. And Jack's eyes still burned straight ahead.

"Why did he hit you?" Frank asked.

"He don't like me much."

"But he doesn't know you."

"He don't have to know me. He just has to look at me. Look at this."

Jack's voice grew hotter as he shot his hands up to draw our attention to the color of his skin.

"That's reason enough."

And then he looked at us. Not to see us, but to judge us.

"And he's a cop, and that's what cops do."

I knew we were no longer with Jack. He had pushed us away. Put us with the cop, with all whites, all the people he hated at this very moment. And the moment hung there like a curtain, separating us.

"Not all cops," I whispered.

"Don't bet your silver dollar on it."

We didn't speak again for some time. The sounds of the subway were all we heard. At least on the outside. Inside, I could hear everything Jack was thinking. All the rage, all the resentment, all building over a lifetime and looking for a place to go. And he alone trying to hold it back from spilling over.

"What's it like?" I asked as softly as I could.

"What?"

"Bein' colored."

Jack turned to me. I could see the feelings and emotions inside of him did something to his face. It made it look older.

"You ever think about you bein' white?"

"No." I said.

"Well a colored man's always think' 'bout his bein' colored 'cause everyone around him is thinkin' 'bout it."

"How do you know what other people is thinkin'?" Frank asked.

"Just know is all."

Jack turned straight ahead once more and let his eyes fix on a spot across the subway car.

"Was a time I didn't know, didn't give it a thought. Wasn't any older than you two."

Jack was leaving. I could see it. There was a place that called to him, called him back, the way the diner called me. And his voice went soft as he spoke. And his eyes never left the empty spot across the car.

"One day I was helpin' my pa at the warehouse where he worked. We was carryin' some boxes outside for this white man while he took a piss. We was carryin' them to his car. Only the man didn't tell us his boys were waitin' in the car for him."

Jack's eyes left the spot across the car and looked down at his feet. The same way they did when speaking to the cop on the platform.

"When they seen my pa comin' toward them, they went out of their minds. Started screamin' and cryin'. Lockin' the doors and windows as fast as they could."

I caught Frank's eye when Jack spoke these words and I knew both of us were thinking about our drive down Williamsbridge Road, locking up our car as we looked out over the black neighborhood.

"I remember my pa, standin' outside that car, lookin' at these boys starin' back at him, scareder than hell, climbin' all over each other tryin' to get away from him like he was gonna kill 'em and eat 'em for supper. Like he wasn't human. And all that time, my pa standin' there in front of his own boy. Knowin' his own boy's watchin' how white people sees him. Like he's an animal."

Then Jack turned to Frank. "Yeah, I know what they're thinkin'. They're all screamin'. Some folks just better at hidin' it."

He turned away from us. And I remember wondering if he'd turned away for the last time. If he was never coming back. If whatever tie existed between us, no matter how tenuous and weak, had been severed.

But there was something I wanted to know.

"You ever wish you were white?"

"No." Jack took a breath. "I wish everybody was colored . . . now shut your mouth and let me be."

And we poured into the darkness of the next tunnel in silence as loud as the thundering wheels that carried us.

Chapter *Eleven*

My mother stood at the window in our living room staring into the street. She'd been standing in the same spot for twenty minutes. Looking for my Uncle Pat, waiting for him to drive up so they could race to the west Bronx. And waiting is never easy. She knew the more she watched the pot the slower it would boil. But this concerned her sons and she needed to get to them. Nothing was going to pull her focus from that single, all-consuming fact. No piece of action was going to clear her mind. Her children were out there and she needed to get to them. So she stood at the window, staring into the street, and waited for my uncle.

Frank and I had learned that we were not capable of taking care of ourselves. That we needed help. Needed someone to take control and keep us safe. My mother had learned that she could be helpless. Not all the time, not on all matters, but at moments, and, as is so often the case, moments which matter most. She learned there are situations that send your mind and body screaming to take control, but circumstances strike against you and you are at the mercy of providence.

My mother would occasionally tell a story which occurred during her childhood. She was twelve and had traveled with my grandparents to Lake Mahopac in upstate New York. It was a small community with heavily-wooded forests and a beautiful lake at its center. It was a favorite spot for families and during the summer months many would flock to its shores. On the first day of the trip they were bathing along the north bank when a young girl jumped into the water from a tree limb extending over the lake. She did not come up. Twenty seconds passed and the girl's mother, realizing something was wrong, raced into the water. What she found was her daughter's foot trapped in a nest of tree branches at the bottom of the lake. The branches clutched her ankle with fierce determination and the more the girl struggled the tighter the grip became.

The lake at that spot was only five feet deep, but the girl was four and a half feet tall. Her mouth, desperate for air, was four inches from the surface. She could see the sky, but couldn't reach it. Witnessing the panic filling her daughter's eyes, the girl's mother pulled with all her strength. She screamed for help, and help came, but the girl was never able to get free of the grip of the trees. Her mother was helpless against nature. And the girl drowned with her face less than a foot from her mother's.

My mom would tell this story and say she could think of no worse thing. No greater pain. To watch your child die before your eyes and be helpless to save them is the greatest torture imaginable. I'm certain she was thinking of that story as she stared out the window.

But there was one thing she could do. She could stop waiting. She could go after her children on her own. My mother turned sharply from the window, marched across the living room, and hurried out the door. Maybe she didn't know exactly where her children were, maybe being at Yankee Stadium wouldn't bring them there any faster or keep them safe on their journey, but that's where they were going and that's where she would be as fast as possible.

She ran to the Cutlass still parked at the curb where Sal had replaced the blown tire. She swung open the driver's side door and was about to slide in when she was startled by the blast of a siren. She turned and saw a police cruiser racing up. At the sight of it, her skin went cold and her knees buckled as all the worst her mind could conjure rushed to the fore.

The cruiser stopped and the passenger door opened and Uncle Pat stepped out.

"What happened?" My mother said with what little air remained in her lungs.

"Nothing happened," Uncle Pat assured her. "It's okay."

"What the hell, Pat?!" She screamed as the tears came again with an outpouring of relief. "What the hell?"

"I'm sorry."

The driver's door opened and a uniformed cop stepped out. It was my father's partner. His name was Jim Halloran.

"Carol. Pat just asked me to come along. Everything's still okay."

My mother shut the door to the Cutlass and rushed over to the cruiser.

"Let's just get over there now," she said as she climbed into the police car.

As far back as I can remember, subways always had the same effect on me. And this time was no different. So despite the fact that we sat in stony silence and Jack was filled with anger and a rift had been plowed between us that might never get repaired, I needed to act.

"I've got to go to the bathroom."

I know I said the words aloud. I'm certain of it because of the drain it had on my being simply to muster the courage to speak them. But you wouldn't know it from the silence that greeted them.

"I have to go," I said with more urgency, because the situation was becoming more urgent.

"We got a few more stops before we get off. Then you can go."

Silence returned and I resolved to hold on until we got to where we were going.

My resolve lasted eighteen seconds.

"I have to go bad."

Jack eyed me.

"Number two," I said.

"Jesus Christ, boy."

"I'm sorry."

"Can't you hold it?"

"He can't hold it," Frank said. "One time he crapped his pants in the car on the way home from school."

"Did not."

"Did too."

"Did not."

"Too."

"Not."

"Enough!" Jack bellowed.

"But he did. Stunk so bad we had to open the windows in the middle of a snowstorm. Freezin' cold it was with snowflakes big as baseballs flying all over the place. Debbie Balma was ridin' with us with her brother Ronnie and she got pneumonia."

"You're a liar!" I shouted with the extra volume of someone who knows the truth is being spoken and wants to discredit it.

"You are!" Frank asserted, knowing it to be the case.

"You are!"

"I'm rubber and you're glue, everything you say bounces off me and sticks on you."

"You're an idiot!" I said, running out of ammo.

"You just called yourself an idiot cause it bounced off me and stuck on you."

"Give it a rest, Frank," Jack said.

Frank gave it rest, but not before laughing that laugh. And this time, I wasn't grateful, and I did want to bash his head in with a big stick.

"All right," Jack said. "I gotta go myself. We'll get off the next stop and find you a toilet. Can you hold your mud that long?"

"Yeah."

"Bet he can't."

"Can so."

"Can not."

"You two is gettin' on my last nerve. I'm sayin', my last goddamn nerve."

We sat quiet. For a moment.

"Bet we're knee deep in crap before the train stops," Frank said. "Bet a dollar."

"Bet your brain is full of crap right now," I countered. "Bet a dollar."

"Jesus Christ and his Mother Mary of Bethlehem but you two ain't like a couple of old married folks. And you ask me how come I don't want no company."

Jack sat grumbling and fidgeting. Frank and I sat quietly, but I glanced over and Frank held his nose and made a face like he was smelling limburger cheese. He got a good look at my tongue in return.

The train finally pulled to a stop and Jack stood.

"Let's go find a toilet."

The doors opened and we stepped out onto the platform.

"Where is it?" I pleaded.

Jack looked around and spotted a sign for the men's room just past the turnstiles.

"Over there."

We quick-stepped across the platform, hurried into the bathroom, and stopped in our tracks. The floor was covered with a foot water colored and filled with turds and urine. A result of the toilets having been blown up with M-80s, I guessed.

"Holy crap," Frank said covering his mouth and nose.

"Ain't nothin' holy about it. A person could choke to death in here."

"Smells like Lucy Longo's locker." Frank said.

"Who?"

"She's gotta take all kinds of medicine on account she's sick and it makes her teeth brown and her locker stink," I added.

"And you had to share it with her," Frank laughed.

"Shut up."

"Both of you shut up," Jack said.

He looked over the horrific sight in front of us.

"I pity the man that's gonna clean this up. Come on."

Jack led us out of the bathroom and back onto the platform.

"We gotta get on the next train when she comes."

"No." I pleaded.

"We'll get off the next stop and find a toilet that ain't all blowed up."

"I gotta go now."

Jack looked at me squeezing my legs and butt with every ounce of strength I had.

"All right. We'll go up top, find a toilet then come back down."

"Bet he don't make it," Frank said.

"Shut up!" Jack barked. "No more back and forth, you hear me. And I want no dilly-dallyin' up there. It's gettin' late and they're just lookin' for a reason to fire a man my age."

We hurried up the stairs as fast as we could, which wasn't very fast, as I had to keep my legs pinned together. But when we reached the street, we were in a different world. A white world. Jack paused a second and looked around warily.

"Maybe best we go back and get . . ."

"I gotta go now, right now."

It was getting serious.

"All right."

Jack checked the buildings and pointed to a restaurant across the street.

We made our way through traffic and entered the bistro. When we did, the crowd turned to look at us. It didn't register to Frank or me so much, but it did to Jack, because that's whom they were staring at. And I could see it made him feel like we felt standing in the street outside Dizzy's Diner.

"Let's go," Jack said when he spotted the owner coming towards us.

He steered us back outside onto the sidewalk.

"What about the bathroom?"

"Not here."

"Why not?" Frank said. "They got one for sure."

"What are you talkin' about, why not?! Didn't you see what was goin' on in there? They don't want no colored man comin' in there. Touchin' their sink. Dryin' his hands on their towels. Draggin' his butt cheeks across their toiled seats."

"But I can't wait!"

"Then you go in!"

The door of the restaurant swung open and the owner, a tall white-haired man, stood in the doorway.

"I can't have you hanging around out front so get moving."

"I ain't hangin'." Jack said. "Boy just had to go to the bathroom is all."

The owner could see I was ready to explode.

"The boy can come in. He'll meet you down at the corner."

"You don't tell me where to go," Jack said firmly. "I go where I please."

"I don't give a damn where you go as long as it's not in front of my place."

The owner stepped sideways leaving room for me to enter.

"Come on, kid."

I looked at Jack as I squeezed my legs.

"Go ahead," Jack said. "I'll meet you down on the corner."

Then he turned to Frank.

"And you go with him. Don't wanna be stoppin' every two minutes."

Frank and I hurried into the restaurant and I heard the owner speak to Jack before he closed the door.

"Get movin' or I'm callin' the cops."

Then he turned toward us and pointed down the hallway.

"Down there on your right."

He didn't have to say it twice. Within a matter of seconds I was inside the bathroom and into a stall. Frank wasn't far behind and took up residence beside me as the first wave of relief washed over me. But with my mind clear now clear, I found myself thinking about what Jack had just said.

"Frank?" I called under the divider toward the stall on my right.

"I ain't falled in," Frank answered.

"Why don't they want Jack touchin' the sink and stuff?"

"I don't know. 'Cause they figure they're gonna catch somethin' from him maybe."

We sat quietly save for the occasional disturbance of the water beneath us.

"You think he's got something to catch?"

"No. I don't know. Would you let me take a crap here?"

I let him take his crap but I was almost finished with mine and wanted some answers.

"Maybe it's cooties."

"It ain't cooties, ya dumb banana. There's no such thing as cooties. That's a make-believe thing."

"I know. So maybe it's a make-believe thing they say he's got that's catchin' so he can't use the sink. Like when you told Greg Sanza we had melotopis so he couldn't eat our ice cream even though there ain't no such thing."

It was quiet. Then I heard Frank drop one and pull on the toilet paper roll.

"Maybe."

"But then why don't they want him using the sink?

"Cause he's a Negro and that's all there is to it." We heard from outside our stalls.

While I can't say for sure about Frank, I know I froze solid. And I'm fairly sure Frank did too, as I didn't hear a sound from his stall. After a moment I got my arms to move and pulled the last sheets of paper off my roll.

"Frank?" I whispered.

"Yeah?" He whispered back.

"I'm out of paper."

Then I heard Frank laugh. Not the other laugh, the epidermis laugh, this one was far more sinister. This laugh says I've got you by the shorthairs.

"Twenty-five cents a square," Frank offered.

"Frank."

"Might be thirty in a couple seconds."

"Here," said the same unknown voice from outside the stall.

I looked straight ahead and saw an old black hand reaching under the door with a roll of fresh toilet paper. I just looked at it when I heard the voice again.

"You ain't afraid it's got cooties? Or meloctopus, or whatever it was you said?"

Then I heard a laugh and the hand shook from the authenticity of it.

I grabbed the roll.

"Thanks."

"My pleasure."

I did the paperwork, flushed at the same time as Frank, and both of us stepped out of our stalls, where we saw a short black man around eighty.

"Name's Vince. Hope you didn't mind me inviting myself into your conversation."

Then it dawned on me. The way he spoke. His accent. He was not American. Frank figured it out as well.

"Where you from?" Frank asked.

"Kenya."

"Where's that?" I asked.

"Africa."

"How'd you get here?" Frank followed up.

"By boat."

"You were a slave?" Frank said.

"I'm not that old," Vince let out a laugh. "I came to America ten years ago to be with my daughter. She's an English teacher."

He turned on the faucets for two of the sinks and held up a dispenser of soap. Frank and I cupped our hands and he gave us each a dollop.

"One and two. Now wash thoroughly."

We scrubbed our hands and gave them a good, hot rinse.

"That why they let you in here?" I asked. "Cause you're not an American colored but an African colored?"

"They let me in because I work here. The other makes no difference."

He handed each of us a warm towel.

"You work in a bathroom?" Frank said, dumb-founded.

"Yes, sir. I keep the items fully stocked. Cologne, gum, brushes, toilet paper."

"Doesn't it smell bad?" I asked.

"It did with you two in there." He smiled a big smile. "But not as bad as the unemployment line. You can toss the towels in that basket."

We did as he instructed.

"Do they let you use the toilet and the sink and stuff?" Frank asked.

"No, they don't."

"Even though you're already in here?"

"Even though I'm already in here."

"And the toilet's right there?"

"And the toilet's right there."

"So what do you do if you have to go?" I asked, now interested in the particulars of his job regulations.

"I use the toilet behind the kitchen."

"Doesn't make sense with a toilet right here."

"I'm in complete agreement with you. But that's the way the paper comes off the roll."

Vince smiled that smile again. It was a quality of smile that made you smile just to see it. It was real and honest and full of love.

"Okay, gentlemen."

He reached to the counter and picked up a tray filled with small bottles of cologne.

"What'll it be today, Brut or English Leather?"

Chapter Twelve

Using his top lights and siren, Officer Halloran tried his best to weave through stand-still traffic. A mile ahead two tow trucks tried to clear the wreckage of a four car pile-up. He glanced over at my mom and could see she was nervous.

"My girls ran away once."

My mom looked over.

"They were ten years old and were mad because we wouldn't let them date boys in their class. They were missing for five hours, so I know what you're feeling."

"Where were they?" My mother asked.

"We found them sleeping in the tool shed in the yard."

"What did you do?"

"Nothing. We put them in bed, kissed them on the cheek, and never said a word about it."

"Boys are different," Uncle Pat said. "And this situation is different. You ask me what they need is a little less coddling and a little more discipline."

"They're babies, Pat," Officer Halloran said. "You forget it and they'll forget it too."

"They're not gonna forget. And it's time they grew up."

"Grew up?" My mother was seething now. "Just think for a second what these kids have been through. What Mickey has been through."

"I appreciate that . . ."

"Appreciate it? Their childhood ended that day! Ended at seven years old!"

"All I'm saying . . ."

"Don't talk to me, Pat. Don't say another word."

My mother turned and stared out at the traffic jam and the crumpled cars being dragged off the road.

"Christ Jim, can you get us through this or what?!"

Frank and I left the restaurant and began making our way toward the far corner where Jack said we should meet him.

"Don't smell like leather," I said, sniffing my hands and the front of my shirt.

"When I start shaving I'm gonna wear Brut all the time and nothing else," Frank said.

"How come?"

"Joe Namath wears Brut."

"Me too. I'm gonna wear Brut."

"You can't wear Brut if I'm wearin' Brut, you gotta wear somethin' else."

We walked a bit farther.

"What'd dad wear again? It was in a white bottle I think, with a cork or somethin' in the top," I said.

"Old Spice. Dad was an Old Spice man. That'd be a good one for you to wear."

"Yeah, I'll be an Old Spice man."

We heard a quick wail of a siren and looked up to see a patrol car bully its way through an intersection. In the back of the car I noticed two young black men with their arms cuffed behind their backs.

"You think Dad ever hit guys?" I asked Frank.

"Sure."

"Yeah, you think?"

"All cops gotta hit guys so they don't get away with the money."

"No. I mean hit guys for just hittin' 'em. Like the cop who hit Jack with his stick. Jack wasn't tryin' to get away with the money."

Frank thought on it for a few seconds.

"No. Dad never hit no one like that."

We reached the end of the block and stood on the corner in front of a laundromat.

"I don't think so either."

Frank looked inside the laundromat and I snuck a look around the corner, but neither of us caught sight of Jack.

"Where is he?"

Frank suddenly grew agitated, like a switch had been thrown. He ran into the laundry, looked all over, then stormed out and began checking the bordering shops.

"He's gone," Frank blurted out.

He started running farther along the streets of the intersection checking each and every storefront, but there was no sign of Jack.

"He's gone."

"He can't be gone."

"He's gone. He left us. I knew it! I knew he'd leave us!"

Frank's eyes began to well up as we hurried back to the corner, but still there was no Jack. And the city began closing in on us once again. The people on the sidewalks, in the cars filling the roads and looking out windows were mostly white, but it didn't matter. They were strangers in a strange place, a loud, tall, boisterous place, and Frank had reached the end of what he could take.

"He wouldn't leave us," I said.

"Do you see him? Huh?"

"No, but . . ."

"He's gone sure as I'm standin' here!"

"Why would he leave us?"

"Cause everybody leaves!"

And the tears began to tumble from his eyes. It was all coming out right here, right now.

"Nobody ever stays. Nobody. Not ever."

I didn't know what to do. I'd never seen Frank like this. Whenever he was hurt, or embarrassed, or felt awkward, his course of action was to either get angry or get funny. He'd either make a joke or get loud and aggressive. This was neither; this was a boy afraid.

"Maybe he . . ."

"He's gone! He left!"

"Why would he do that?"

"Cause we went in to take a crap and he couldn't. We were allowed to take a crap and he wasn't."

"He left 'cause we took a crap?"

"And 'cause he couldn't. And 'cause we're white and colored people hate white people!"

"And why shouldn't we?"

We turned toward the familiar voice and saw Jack step from behind a garbage bin in the back of a dark alley. He was zipping his fly and buckling his trousers as he walked out of the blackness.

"Why shouldn't a colored man hate a white man?"

He marched toward us until our backs were pinned against the front window of the laundromat.

"You see a colored cop whippin' on a white man? Did a colored man keep you from callin' your mama in the diner? Or let you die right in front of 'em 'cause white folk ain't allowed in a colored hospital? Huh?"

Frank shook his head meekly.

"Did anybody take a bat out of your hand and stick a rake in it? Tell you that you can clean up the crap but you can't play the game cause you're white?"

"No," Frank murmured.

"Damn straight."

We stood silent, not moving. Not Frank, not me, not Jack.

"You think a white man would haul a couple colored boys back to Harlem? Hell, no."

Jack looked straight at Frank.

"Why shouldn't we hate you? You tell me. Why shouldn't we?"

"I don't know."

"Me neither."

It felt like a switch had been flipped in Jack as well. He was colder now. Meaner. With no patience or understanding. And it was more than just the slights and abuses he suffered since we left Dizzy's, it was all of them plus a lifetime of incidents and whispers just like them.

It dawned on me that the reason Jack wanted to be alone, why he didn't want company, why he wanted to walk through the remaining years of his life as a ghost, invisible to everyone, was that he didn't want any more witnesses. He could live with the cruelty and the hatred that targeted him for the color of his skin, but only if no one saw. If it was just him who knew how much he'd been humiliated, how much he had to suffer for the short-comings of others, how low he had to bow his head, he'd be able to swallow it and keep walking. But now we were here. White people. White boys. And he couldn't swallow any more. Now he choked on it. It gagged him, cut off his ability to breathe and made him nauseated. Made him want to strike back. He wasn't going to swallow humil-iation; he wasn't going to swallow dishonor or degradation with children watching. Not anymore.

"Let's go."

He turned and walked with purpose. His stride seemed even longer than before and Frank and I were running to keep up. We cut across the street and turned toward a subway entrance about mid-block.

"Hurry up now!" Jack yelled over his shoulder as Frank and I did all we could to stay at his heels.

We reached the entrance to the subway and tried to weave through a sea of people streaming up from the platform.

"Ain't runnin'," a young black man said to Jack.

"What?"

"Subway ain't runnin."

"Why the hell not?"

"Electrical somethin' or other, I ain't sure. But I'm damn sure it ain't runnin'."

Jack looked like he wanted to tear the banister off the stairwell and throw it as far as he could. He turned toward me and barked.

"Couldn't hold your mud another ten minutes. Ten goddamn minutes and you couldn't hold it."

"I'm sorry."

"Damn right you're sorry. You about the sorriest son-of-a-bitch I've seen. I was on a bus from Memphis to St. Louis with my bowels so bad I thought my head would explode. But I held my ass puckered tight for three hours and twenty-six minutes, across two state lines. 'Cause a man does, and a baby cries. And that's what you are, a baby."

I could see the veins in his neck and forehead bulging. See the blood coursing through them as he tried to bottle the tide rising up within him. And I could feel my own blood, growing hot, shaking inside my veins, pouring into my brain, which was telling me to go away, go to the place you belong. Get out of here right now. It's easy. Just let yourself go. Let it take over your body and mind, and maybe this time you won't come back. You won't have to feel this anymore. You can just stay with your dad. But I fought it. With everything I had.

"You know I'm gonna be late? You know that, don't you?"

I didn't say anything.

"First time in near thirty years. Goddamnit! You know they lookin' for an excuse to get rid of a man near sixty-five years old don't you? Then what am I gonna do? What am I gonna do when I ain't got no job?! I'll tell you what I'm gonna do. I'm gonna live on the street. I'm gonna eat trash out of garbage cans and die froze to a cardboard box in the dead of winter 'cause you couldn't hold your damn mud for ten minutes."

"We can call a cab," Frank said. Weakly, but he said it.

Frank found his strength watching me fall under Jack's assault. Not because he liked it, or was happy the focus was off him, but because he was protective. It was in his nature. His driving force. He stood tall for those he cared about. And not just since my father died, but always. He took a beating for me once.

It was the last summer my dad was alive, and a group of us kids had a fire hydrant open to get cool on a hot, humid day. There were youngsters of all ages in the spray of that water. New York was like that. There were the kids you went to school with, who were mostly your age, and the kids you played with on the block who came in all ranges. Two of the older boys, already in their teens, wanted the frogman scuba mask my parents had given me for my seventh birthday. It didn't work well, fogging up and filling with water every time it got near water, even the bathtub, but it was mine, and I wanted to wear it into the streams of water rushing from the hydrant. One of the boys grabbed hold of me and the other tried to pull it off my face. But I held on with all I had and still had it in my hand when I hit the ground with my lip cut and nose bloodied. The two teens moved toward me and readied for the worst when Frank stepped in between us. There were seven other kids there, but not one stepped in to help Frank. I kept my scuba mask.

"Cab?" Jack scoffed. "You got any money for a cab?"

"My mom'll pay for it when we get there."

"Don't matter who's gonna pay for it. Ain't gonna find a cabbie that's gonna pick up a colored man anyhow."

"How . . . ?"

"And don't be askin' me how come 'cause you know damn well how come. You been watchin' how come for the better part of the day."

Jack stood lookin' around, searching for answers.

"Don't know what the hell I'm doin' here in the first place. Ain't none of my goddamn business. I'm sick of this. Sick of all of it. Of all of you. Take a man's skin and bones and it still ain't enough, gotta have his soul too. Well I ain't givin' no more. I'm takin' now. And I know where I'm gonna start. Let's move."

Jack started walking south and Frank and I again followed at top speed.

"We lookin' for a new subway?" Frank asked.

"Don't you worry what we're lookin' for, you just keep your mouth shut and your legs movin'."

"But where we goin'?"

Jack stopped and turned on Frank.

"One more word out of you and you're gonna find yourself all alone out here. In the dark. With all the things that live in the dark. So you just shut your mouth and don't concern yourself where we're goin'."

He turned and continued on. As did Frank and I, except we were quiet this time.

Chapter Thirteen

Twenty minutes had passed. Twenty minutes since my mother, Uncle Pat, and Officer Halloran entered the maintenance offices at Yankee Stadium.

"I don't know what to tell you," said the middle-aged supervisor whose pale skin and undernourished body reflected his preference for desk over field work. "He should've been here ten minutes ago."

My mother's eyes combed the security cameras that occupied one wall and provided black-and-white video feed of the ballpark.

"Maybe he called, spoke to someone else?" Uncle Pat asked.

"No. I'm the only one in the office tonight. Rest of the crew is on site."

The supervisor pointed to the television screens, which showed several other members of the maintenance team working in various locations around the stadium.

"Does he generally call if he's running behind?" asked Officer Halloran.

"He never runs behind. He's been on time, if not early, for as long as I've been here and that's seventeen years."

"Something's happened. I know it," my mother said. "Something's wrong."

"I'm sure everything's all right,." the supervisor replied. "Jack's a . . ."

"Don't tell me everything's all right. He hasn't been late in fifteen years but today he's late? The day he's got my kids? You understand that? He's got my babies."

"But not as a representative of the New York Yankees."

My mother wanted to split him open with an ax, which came as no surprise to Uncle Pat or Officer Halloran.

"No one's saying anything about the Yankees. We're just trying to find these boys," Halloran said. "Let me see his employee card."

"What do you want it for?"

"I'm going to call in his description so officers in the field can be on alert."

"An APB?" Uncle Pat asked.

"No. They haven't been gone long enough and you willingly placed them in his custody. But we can get a lot of eyes out there and see what they can see."

"I would need to call upstairs and get authority for something like that and I'm not sure anyone is..."

"You don't give him that employee card right now," my mother said, "and something happens to my children, so help me god I'll spend my last dime making it the responsibility of the New York Yankees."

The supervisor looked at the intensity in my mother's face and knew she wasn't bluffing. He pulled Jack's information card from a rolodex and handed it to Officer Halloran, who was already dialing the phone.

My mother heard him speak, but her focus and her mind were on the tv screens and the parking lots and the entrances and her children.

"Something's wrong." My mother whispered under her breath. "Something's wrong."

We walked at top speed for over twenty blocks. Turning left, turning right, then left once again and so on till Frank and I had no idea which way we were going. Not that we had a chance to discuss it as it took every ounce of strength we possessed to keep pace with Jack, who ate up the city with purposeful strides. He was on a mission, there was no mistake about that. What it was, and where we were going, was a mystery. I had no idea what he had in mind or where he was taking us except for the certainty that it was not Yankee Stadium.

Some of the streets we walked, the buildings we passed, were familiar. I remembered seeing them during the bus drive from camp. We had traveled these same streets when we crossed the Lincoln Tunnel. And while I didn't know the city at all, I did know Yankee Stadium was in the Bronx, and Jack was taking us in the opposite direction.

We cut through a large, indoor, parking lot, climbed down from level two to level one, and emerged onto a crowded sidewalk. Jack led us to the crosswalk and we waited for a green light with a mixture of men and women, many of whom wore white labcoats over their clothes.

"We're not goin' over there are we?" Frank asked in disbelief.

Across the street, occupying a full city block, was an enormous building with wide glass doors which opened automatically. Above the entrance read the sign, City General Hospital.

"Yes," Jack answered.

"Why're we goin' in there?" I asked, as a hint of alarm crept into my voice.

"Cause I need to do somethin'."

"He doesn't like hospitals; you can't take him in there." Frank informed him.

"I've heard all I care to hear about what he likes and don't like. I got somethin' to do in there and I'm gonna do it. You understand?"

Jack then took us both by the arm, held us in place and brought his face close to ours.

"We're gonna go in there and I'm gonna do the talkin', and I don't want to hear a peep out of either of you. No matter what I say. Even if you think it ain't true or don't understand it, you just keep your mouths shut. You don't say nothin' to nobody about what I say. You just stand there like nice white boys and if any of 'em look at you, you just nod. You understand?"

"Yeah, but Mickey can't go in there." Frank was trying to make him understand. "He gets sick in a place like that, and it's bad, so you can't take him in there."

"I don't want to hear it." Jack turned to me. "Whatever you're scared of, you just get over it and stay quiet."

The light turned green and Jack took us by the hand and walked briskly across the street. We approached the front doors, but even before they opened I could smell it. Alcohol and disinfectant. Disease and sickness. I could smell it all. I could smell death. It was so strong, so all-consuming, I didn't even notice all the white faces staring at Jack as he led us inside.

The main lobby was crowded with the sick and the grieving. And my body tensed with each step we took deeper inside the building. But Jack kept us moving. Past the waiting area filled with the elderly, past the entrance to the Emergency Room where a bloody stretcher sat unattended, and past the security guard who kept his eyes on Jack from the moment we stepped foot in his territory. We marched toward the front desk, but before we reached it, Jack stopped and turned to us.

"You stay here and don't say nothin'."

We waited and Jack approached the receptionist with a softer demeanor, almost apologetic.

"What are we doing here?" I whispered to Frank.

"I don't know, maybe he knows somebody who's here, somebody sick."

"No, he wasn't comin' here. We were goin' to the Stadium. He just decided all of a sudden."

"I don't know."

I could see Frank take a closer look at me and I suppose he didn't like what he saw because he tried to console me.

"Just . . . I don't know, think about somethin' else, all right. Don't get all crazy or nothin'."

"See what he's sayin'," I said to Frank.

Frank quietly stepped closer. I stepped with him.

". . . the boys' papa is here." I heard Jack say. "Up on the fourth floor, Room 410, no 412—no, 410—I can never remember."

"What's he sayin' that for?"

Jack heard my voice and turned with a look that froze me in my place.

"Mr. Chambers?" The receptionist asked.

"Yes, Mr. Chambers. I work for him and he asked me to bring the boys for a visit. So I brought them."

The woman looked past Jack and set her eyes upon Frank and me. We didn't say a word. We were too scared. She checked her records once more. I could see Jack shifting his weight from foot to foot and I knew he was anxious.

You can bring them up, Room 410," she said as she handed Jack a pass. "Just sign here."

Jack signed his name. "Thank you."

He turned and took our hands once more.

"Come on, boys."

He walked us toward the elevators.

"Why'd you say my dad was here? Why'd you say that?" I asked urgently.

"You just shut your mouth."

Jack kept walking, taking a moment to let go of Frank's hand so he could hold up his pass to the security guard who'd made his way from the front door to take a closer look at Jack.

"Just takin' the boys up to see their pa."

The guard didn't question Jack, who reached out and pressed the call button for the elevator.

I wanted to say something. To make this, whatever this was, stop. I wanted to leave, I wanted to get out. But the doors opened and Jack led us inside. And the security guard followed.

Jack pressed the button for the fourth floor and the four of us rode quietly. The guard never took his eyes off Jack, who kept his head bowed like he did with the cop on the subway platform. We rode beyond the first floor and then the second. Not a word was spoken. And then the guard reached out and hit the button for the third floor. The car came to an immediate halt. The doors opened and the guard walked out, leaving the elevator to us, and us alone.

When the door closed, Jack reached out and hit the button for the seventh floor, which was listed on the panel as Executive Offices.

"I thought we were going to the fourth floor?" Frank asked.

"I got someone I need to see on the seventh."

And with that I saw Jack covertly slide something from his pocket. He kept it tucked in his palm and partially concealed by his sleeve, but I could still see it. Still knew what it was. It was a knife. And then I knew, Jack meant to hurt someone. To kill them, maybe. I didn't know why. I didn't understand his motive, but I knew just the same. He came here because someone had hurt him and he was going to repay the debt.

The elevator slowed as we approached the fourth floor. I could feel my legs and arms vibrating, my skin burning. Jack was going to kill someone on the seventh floor, I was sure of it. My breath grew labored and I had to struggle to pull air into my lungs. *Jack is going to kill somebody* kept running through my brain, over and over; it was all I could hear.

The car came to a stop, the doors opened, and I shot out like a horse breaking from the starting gate. I pushed through an older couple waiting to board the elevator and kept running.

"Mickey!"

It was Jack calling me, but I was running now, getting away. I was trapped by this moment, by my life, by everything around me, and I had to escape. Heads began turning and voices yelled for me to stop running but I kept moving. Down the hall, and all the while behind me, chasing me, calling me back, was Jack and Frank and the coffee shop—the coffee shop—the coffee shop.

I hit the exit door at the far end of the hall and everything went black. The darkness dropped like an anvil and I was in the void, the waiting room for the truth I had to face. Once and for all. And not the truth as I wanted it to be. But the truth as I knew it to be. All of it. Buried deep so I could survive, so I could take one more step, one more breath. But its time had come. The fear brought me along slowly, but it was ready. It wanted me to look into its fire and be consumed by it.

I felt a thud as I hit the ground, my head banging off the top stair as my body tumbled like a rag doll to the landing below. End-over-end I flew, but it didn't matter. Whatever pain it supplied me was nothing compared to what was waiting.

I was lying in a heap when I heard the door at the top of the stairwell open.

"Mickey!" Jack cried out.

"Oh god!" Frank shouted.

Then the sound of footsteps coming quickly down the metal stairs, coming to help me, but they were too late. I was gone. I was there.

It was a glorious day to be sure. The sun pouring through the windows. Air made crisp and clean by winter's cool breeze. And our breakfasts. My father's and mine. Filling us with more than nourishment, filling us with love. It was a great day. The kind of day that fills you with the certainty that anything and everything is possible. That what lies beyond the curve of the road is good. That light always follows darkness. That people are in fact, kind. It was a glorious day. But it wasn't really a day, it was just a moment. One that was about to end, and end everything else along with it.

When I return to this coffee shop I'm able to look around, to see and hear things. I'm not tied to the thoughts that filled me as I sat beside my father that Sunday in December. I'm able to move around like a ghost, to notice more, feel more of the experience.

I could see the elderly couple sitting quietly in the corner, the man waiting patiently as his wife cut his ham steak into small, manageable pieces. He would later tell investigators one of the gunmen had a hole in his jacket through which he saw a sweatshirt containing the word "state", though he couldn't be sure if it was all of a word or part of a word. There was the young mother and her three-year-old twins. They sat directly behind us, busy with

Crayola Crayons and coloring books depicting the stories of Mother Goose. She remembered nothing except pulling her daughters under the table when the shooting started, she never even saw the gunmen. And there was the waitress who flirted with me and called me "Sir" when she stopped by to see if our food was satisfactory.

"Are the pancakes to your liking, sir?"

It's only now, on these subsequent visits, that I realize she wasn't flirting with me, but with my father. She was standing directly in front of us, offering him a wink, when the three young men charged into the shop.

And this time, this visit, I see it. Just before the men broke the glass of the front door, I had sipped my chocolate milk. I took an extra big gulp because I'd packed a larger than normal amount of pancake into my mouth, and I wanted to make sure I got it all down. I wiped some residue from my chin with my left forearm and . . .

Then everything stops. A moment frozen in time. The last moment. The last moment of the life I'd been living.

Slowly it starts up, moving like single images from the pages of a scrapbook. My father reaching for his gun. The busboy emerging from the kitchen with a mop. My father spinning as he holds up his badge. The fire truck driving past the side window as I turn to see what's happening. My father rising out of his seat, gun pointed, and yelling, "POLICE!" as I first see the young men with their guns and masks. And the arrival of the fear. Crushing, paralyzing fear.

I try to stop this from playing out. I don't want to be here any longer. I don't want to see the next part. But I do see it. All of it. I see the thing I've blocked from my memory with every ounce of strength I possess. I see the glass of chocolate milk slip from my hand.

"Please, god, no."

I beg my fingers to close, for the muscles in my hand to respond to my prayers and force my grip to tighten before the rim of the glass passes through into thin air. But it doesn't tighten. I can't close my small, weak fingers. And I watch the glass fall, and fall, and fall. Seconds go by, hours go by, a lifetime goes by, and then the glass shatters to the floor with a sickening crash.

My father's head snaps around at the jarring sound and his eyes fix on mine. And I see it. The moment of realization when he knows the sound he heard was my glass falling from my hand, falling from my clumsiness, or lack of focus, like the milk bottles I broke in our car, providing a stench we would live with from that moment on. I saw all of this flash in his eyes. And I saw him realize that his death was only an instant away. I see it as he looks into my face. It was me. I killed him.

Then the bullets come, and the explosion of sound, and the splattering of my father's flesh across my face. I live all of it again. The chaos, the panic, the screaming, and my father's lifeless body slumped on the ground, pressed against the foot-rail, his blood pooling beneath my feet. Only it isn't blood. It's chocolate milk. My chocolate milk. And my hand is still in front of me, shaped as though I was still holding the glass. But the hand is empty. As am I.

"Daddy's here. Mickey. Daddy's here."

Could it be him? Could he be calling me? After what I've done. After I've killed him. Is he calling me to join him? Does he still want me?

"Mickey, it's okay. Daddy's here."

Please be so, please be so, please be so. I close my eyes and say those words over and over as I let myself go. Away from this place. Away from the pain. And to my father.

"Daddy's here. Come on boy. Come on."

I felt my eyes flutter then open. But before I could see, I could feel. I felt my body ache from the fall down the metal stairs. I felt my hands clenched in balled up fists, my teeth cutting against one another, and my spine locked firm and rigid. Then slowly my vision cleared, my eyes were able to focus, and I looked into Jack's face as he held me in his arms.

"It's okay. You're okay. I got ya. I got ya."

At the sight of him my body recoiled and snapped back like a taut wire. I was scared of Jack. Still convinced he was going to hurt someone. But he hung onto me, kept me tight in his strong embrace.

"It's okay, you're all right. Ain't nothin' gonna happen to you, or nobody, I promise."

I continued to struggle, but I was weak. The visit to the coffee shop drained me as it always drained me. Forcing me to leave a piece of my soul each time I came back. And all those pieces were leaving me empty. I continued to struggle, but my eyes closed, and slowly I slipped into unconsciousness as I heard Jack repeat over and over.

"I got ya. I got ya. I got ya."

Chapter Fourteen

Nothing had been said for some time. Not since Officer Halloran spoke to Jack's sister and learned we had left for the Stadium two hours prior. The four of them sat in the office waiting. Not knowing what to say. It should have taken twenty minutes, maybe thirty if the subways ran late, but two hours had passed. Two hours. So they sat silent and let their minds go where they would inevitably go. My mother didn't even try to block the fears from entering. She knew there was no use in it. She knew whatever hope she could muster to push the dark thoughts from her mind would be too weak. It would crack and crumble into dust.

Hope can be a powerful weapon against despair, against anxiety, against fear, but it's also susceptible to the eroding qualities of pain and suffering. My mother's hope had been destroyed by a knock on the door seven months earlier. Officer Halloran knew this, as he was the one who had knocked. When the worst that can happen, happens, it kills hope, because hope is faith, and you've now seen the Devil. You can no longer convince yourself he doesn't exist, that he won't show his hand to you, because you've already felt its hot sting. So you sit quietly and let your mind go where it will go.

I woke in the dark. It took some time for my eyes to adjust, but I could hear the faint sound of music. R&B music. It was drifting up through the floorboards. Slowly, I came to realize I was lying on a cloth-covered couch. And the couch was in an old, cluttered office. In my hand was my father's coin. I'd been clutching it so hard, President Eisenhower's profile was imprinted into my palm. Then I saw Frank sitting in the big leather chair behind the desk.

"You all right?" Frank asked.

I nodded.

"Where are we?"

"Some bar or somethin'." Frank said. "He carried you like fifteen blocks. You don't remember?"

"No."

"He tried to get a cab, but like he said nobody would stop. So he started runnin' with you. I said, why don't we get a bus? But he never said nothin', just kept runnin', he was pretty freaked out."

"Where is this place?"

"Kinda back where we started, I'm not sure, we was runnin' so hard I didn't have time to look where we was goin'."

We sat quietly. But the silence was too loud.

"You hear that music?" Frank said.

"Yeah."

"There's a bar down there. They're all dancin' like on tv. You know that show we saw with all the colored people dancin'. You can see it through the vent if you want."

I shook my head, no. Then more quiet came until Frank finally asked what he wanted to ask for seven months.

"What are you thinkin' about when it happens?"

I looked over at Frank and I could see he wasn't asking out of blind curiosity, or some morbid need to hear the details of our father's murder. He was asking because he wanted to know what I was feeling and why I was feeling it. I could see he wanted to connect with me. The type of connection we'd had for so many years but was taken from us that day. He was seeking a way in and offering me a way out, not unlike my mother tried to do in the kitchen. But I still wasn't ready, still didn't have the courage.

"Just that day."

"I know, but what about it?"

I shrugged. "Just stuff."

"Like what?"

"Like just stuff."

We heard the door open and turned to see Jack standing in the frame.

"How you feelin'?" he asked.

I shrugged and Jack approached with a cup of tea.

"This'll make you feel better."

"What is it?" Frank asked.

"Some hot tea."

"You only brought one?" Frank asked.

"It's for your brother."

Jack gently took hold of my arm.

"Come on, sit up."

He then helped me to a sitting position and handed me the cup.

"Go on, drink a bit."

I blew the steam off the surface of the brown liquid and took a small sip. It was cinnamon flavor. My mother drinks the same tea, so I knew it well.

The room was again quiet, except for the soft lilt of Diana Ross singing "I'm Gonna Make You Love Me."

"Scared me pretty damn good back there," Jack said. "Practically had a turd runnin' down my own leg."

Neither Frank nor I said a word.

"But . . . I suppose I scared you pretty good too. And I'm . . . I'm sorry 'bout that."

There was a moment of quiet as Jack searched his mind. He wanted to speak, but it made him uncomfortable. I could tell whatever it was he wanted to say, this type of conversation was foreign to him. Made him self-conscious. So I knew what he had to say had feeling behind it.

"Frank told me about your pa. About what happened. Ain't nobody should have to go through that. Nobody. Especially no young boy. No sir."

Jack took a long look at me.

"You ain't no baby, Mickey. I was wrong to say such a thing. I suppose you lived more'n a lifetime this past year. So I'm sorry what I said. I'm sorry to the both of you. For what I said to ya, and what I was about to do at that hospital. It was wrong. I was wrong. I been takin' out on you two what you had nothin' to do with. You gave me no reason to be like that, but I was, and I'm sorry."

Jack sat his tired body on the steel chair beside the couch.

"Sometimes a man's like a dog that's been beat on. After a while he can't tell the hand that wants to feed him from the hand that wants to hit him, so he ends up just snappin' at both. You understand what I'm sayin' to ya?"

I nodded.

"It's like Ralph D'Ciaocomo," Frank offered.

"Who?"

"This kid from our school. He used to stutter all the time. Way way worse than Mickey. Sometimes it'd take him five minutes just to say his name. Everybody used to make fun of him, so now he just don't talk no more. Teacher'd ask him a question and he'd just sit there like a stone. Tina Tagliarini said he hasn't said one word in almost three years."

"But no one makes fun of him anymore," I said.

Jack took a breath and turned to Frank.

"Frank, why don't you go downstairs and get a Coca-Cola from Janis."

"I'm not thirsty."

"I want to talk to your brother."

"Can't I hear it?"

"Just go get a Coca Cola."

"I'll be quiet. I'll just s . . ."

"Frank."

Frank got up and crossed toward the door.

"I ain't got money for a coke."

"Just tell Janis to put it on my tab."

Frank hesitated a bit longer, hoping for a reprieve from the governor, then walked out.

Jack turned to me.

"I guess you been tryin' to figure out why it happened. Why it happened the way it did."

I nodded.

"I did the same thing after my boy died. And his mother after that. Tried to figure it out. Neither one of them had to die, but they're gone just the same. One on account of this war and one on account of people just hatin' one another for no reason other than the color of their skin. I tried to figure on it, but I couldn't. I couldn't come up with no reason that made no sense. So what'd I do? I just hated more. Just kept it goin.' The very thing that killed my Angela in the first place. And I ask myself why. Why did this have to happen to me? But I ain't come up with an answer yet. And I suspect I never will."

Then something passed over his eyes. A memory. Sweet and bitter.

"My wife used to say everything happens for a reason. That God has his reasons. She was a church-goin' woman. And I was a church-avoidin' man. I don't know, maybe that's why I ain't found no reason yet."

I sipped the tea and let its warmth down inside me as Jack moved his chair closer.

"I think sometimes things happen. Bad things. The worst things. And there ain't no reason. And there ain't no silver lining. It just is what it is. And you got to live with it. But I'm sure of one thing. Your father loved you very much. You and Frank were the most important things in his life and he ain't mad at ya. And he don't blame ya. And he don't want you thinkin' like that. He died protectin' you and the rest of them people in that diner 'cause that's what he believed in."

"But . . . I did it."

"No. No, you didn't. Those men did it. Did you pull a gun? Did ya?"

"No."

"And your pa needs you to understand that. He needs you to live yourself a full life. To grow up and meet a woman, raise children of your own. 'Cause that's how a man lives on. Through his children. And their children. It's what keeps him alive. And if you don't do that and you let yourself get drowned by this, then you are takin' away everything he lived for, and his soul will never be at rest. He needs you to be strong, Mickey."

My hands began to tremble as I felt the emotion try to take hold of me. But I fought it back the way I always did. To feel it was too much. I wasn't ready for that much pain. I wasn't ready for that heavy a load.

Jack took my cup and placed it on the table.

"I just wish he was here," I said in a soft whisper.

Jack took me in his arms and pulled me to him.

"I know you do, boy."

"I miss him."

"I know it. But the Lord gives you the strength to stand, what he gives you to stand. You strong enough for this. You may not know it, but you are. And that don't mean you gotta like it. You go ahead and be mad at God. He loves you and he ain't gonna hold it against you if you tell him what you think. So you holler at him when you need to. You say I'm mad as hell at you for puttin' this on me, you old son-of-a-horse-thief. And you get yourself ready 'cause when it's my turn, I'm comin' up there and I'm gonna kick your ass from one side of Heaven to the other."

"But maybe it wasn't what he wanted to happen."

"Yeah, it is." Jack said.

"But I did somethin' . . . somethin' that made it happen the way it did."

Jack looked at me and his head nodded ever so slightly.

"Hardest thing in life, harder than anything you'll ever know, and it happens to everyone at one time or another, not as young as you but it happens to everyone you can be certain of that . . . and that's knowin' that when a moment came, big or small, for whatever reason, you didn't act like the man you wanna be. The man you see yourself to be. You fell short. The whys, the whats and the how comes don't matter. And it don't matter if it was your fault or not. All you know is you didn't live up to what you had in mind for yourself. How you want to be as a man. And that . . . that'll gnaw at you all the days of your life if you let it."

He took a slow breath and let the words gather in his throat.

"Sometimes, I think back to the day my Angela died and I say to myself, maybe if you ate breakfast instead of skippin' it she would have had her attack at home instead of travelin' to work, been closer to our doctor. Maybe if I showered a little longer, changed my pants one more time, held her in my arms when we woke that mornin', and told her I loved her, any number of things I did or didn't do that made it my fault she's gone. And there ain't nothin' nobody can say to make me feel any different. To take away the responsibility I feel for what happened. Only I can say it to me. And only you can say it to you."

"What do I say?"

"I forgive myself."

I looked at Jack when he said those words because I could see he wasn't just telling me to say them. He was saying them, too.

"And it don't have to be all at once, it couldn't be, it's too big a rock to break in one blow, but a little every day. Every mornin' and every night you whisper to yourself. You say, I forgive myself a little more today. And each day the part you blame yourself for is gonna get less and less until that big 'ol rock is dust and there ain't nothin' left to forgive."

Jack lifted up my chin. "Can you say it?"

I looked into his eyes. I wanted to say it, to believe it, but I couldn't, not yet.

"I know it's hard. Hardest thing you'll ever have to do. But a man ain't what he says, it's what he does. And you gotta be a man now. Your childhood was stolen from you that day. It's wrong and it's sad, but it's true and there ain't no gettin' it back. So you're gonna have to get started bein' a man, Mickey. It's the only way you're gonna survive this."

We heard someone breathing by the door. It was Frank. He stood there with two cokes in his hands. I didn't know how long he'd been there, but I could see in his face that he had heard a great deal of what Jack had to say.

"You want one?" Frank said to me.

I nodded and Frank circled around and handed me a Coke.

Chapter *Fifteen*

We were in the South Bronx and riding quietly in an old bus toward One Hundred Sixty-First Street. Jack figured my mom was pretty worried and had called his boss before we left, but the line was busy. He tried several more times without luck and thought it best we stayed put, but Frank talked him into taking us to Yankee Stadium. He told Jack the phone line could be busy forever and maybe we should get over there and ask Janis of the Coca-Colas if she would mind calling every few minutes and tell 'em we're on our way. I think Jack said yes, because he still felt poorly about what happened at the hospital.

My mind was on everything Jack had said to me, but then I caught sight of the stadium. Big as the biggest building I'd ever seen. I'd never been there at night, only day games, but what was going through my brain was not how amazing the place looked lit up, even though the team was in Baltimore that night, but on something else.

"You figure Ma's there?" I said to Frank.

"Yep."

"You figure he's with her?"

"Yep."

The closer we drove, the bigger the stadium loomed.

"I don't think she's gonna let us stay."

"She might," Frank said.

"I think she's gonna know what we did. I think she's gonna be mad."

"You don't know that."

"This is it," we heard Jack say as he stood from his seat.

The bus slowed, then stopped at the corner. Jack led us down to the sidewalk. We walked quietly toward the stadium when I felt his hand on my shoulder.

"Whatever it is you think is waitin' on you ain't near as bad as you think it is."

We crossed the street and approached the stadium from the north entrance.

"You two ever been to the stadium before?" Jack asked.

"Not at night," Frank said. "We were suppose to go to a night game this year but, well, you know."

I saw Jack steal a glance at Frank.

"We'll get you to a night game," Jack said.

We walked past the ticket booths and entered through Gate 227 and cut down a long dark tunnel.

"Ain't nothin' like Yankee Stadium in all of baseball. Everyone of 'em that's ever put on the spikes wants to play here. I don't care if you're from St. Louis, Cincinnati, or Tokyo, Japan."

"Jack?" I said softly.

"Yeah?"

"Maybe you could go and talk to them first."

"Mickey," Jack said, "there ain't nothin' for you to be afraid of. They love you, both of 'em. And your uncle's only doin' what a man should. Wouldn't you take care of Frank's family if anything happened to him?"

"Frank doesn't have a family."

"I know he ain't got a family, he's nine years old."

"Eight," I corrected.

"I'm eight and ten months so you round up." Frank protested.

"But you're still eight," I said.

"Don't start that up again," Jack said. "I'm just saying if Frank had a family, down the road, a long time from now, and somethin' happened to him, you'd want to do everything you could to help them, right?"

"Yeah."

"That's right. And sometimes what's best ain't the most comfortable or most popular. I take my hat off to your uncle for what he's doin'."

"But you ain't wearin' a hat," Frank reminded.

Jack closed his eyes and shook his head.

"No Frank, I'm not wearin' a hat."

He took hold of the slide gate of a steel fence and rolled it back along its rudder and the three of us emerged onto the outfield grass, which was bathed in light pouring down from heaven above.

"Holy Christmas," Frank gasped as we looked out over the field. "They ain't gonna believe this."

"Who ain't gonna believe it?" Jack asked.

"Nobody."

To stand there was to at once feel larger than life and infinitesimally small. The empty stands that we imagined were filled with cheering fans. The scoreboard lit up to reveal we were embattled in a tie game that would send us to the playoffs. The empty visitor dugout, now filled with enemy combatants wanting to make a stand against the mighty Yankees. All of the fantasies we lived out on the streets of our neighborhood were coming to life in the very place fantasies were born.

"Home plate must be a million miles away," Frank said.

"More like four hundred sixty-five feet," Jack replied. "And you're standin' right were DiMaggio and Mantle stood. Right where your two feet are resting this very second. On those exact blades of grass."

"This is so cool."

And off we went, running across the vast plains of centerfield as if we were Yankees ourselves. And as we ran in the arena of our heroes, all pain, all doubt, all guilt, all of it was gone from our minds. There wasn't room for it. Our hearts and souls were filled with the moment at hand, with the ability, for however short a time, to be someone else.

In the supervisor's office my mother was on the phone with Janis from the nightclub. The phone line wasn't busy forever and she was able to reach my mom and tell her what had happened.

"Thank you so much . . . thank you," my mother said before hanging up.

"What'd she say?" Uncle Pat asked.

"Mickey had a seizure."

"Oh Jesus."

"She said he's okay. The man, Jack, brought him in and spent time with him. Told him his daddy was here."

My mother's eyes began welling up. The pain she endured today was too much and she was losing her strength to fight it.

"Are they still there?" Officer Halloran asked.

"No. They left. They should..."

Then my mother's eyes caught sight of something. In the security cameras occupying the wall next to the supervisor's desk, in the grainy black and white picture, she saw Frank and me running toward second base.

She bolted from the room without a word, pushing past my Uncle Pat with single-purpose determination.

"Carol . . ." Uncle Pat called after her.

But she was gone.

"What the . . ."

"They're here." The supervisor pointed to the screen. And Uncle Pat was out the door.

Frank and I stood on second base, panting, catching our breath, drinking in the moment. The infield dirt like a brown sandy beach beneath our feet as Jack jogged in behind us.

"Think you boys could score on a single?"

"Easy." Frank beamed.

"Last one to home base is eatin' elephant snot on the chicken," I said, and was off like a shot.

"Hey!" Frank called out, but I wasn't stopping.

My legs churned with all the force within them as Frank tried to close the distance.

"You cheated!" He cried out.

I turned the corner at third, driving my inside foot into the bag to keep the turn as tight as possible. I was headed for home now and I could hear the roar of the crowd as I bore down the line. And for an instant, I saw my father sitting in the front row, rising out of his seat to cheer me on. A hot dog falling from his hand and beer sloshing from his cup as I leapt into my slide. Head first, wrapping my arms around home plate. Safe. Safe at last.

Frank slid in right behind me and the two of us lay tangled in a mix of arms, legs, dust, and heroism.

"Mickey!"

I saw my mother running from the Yankees dugout. I barely got to my feet when she scooped me in her arms and squeezed me to her with a force I hadn't felt before. A gush of tears poured from her eyes.

"Don't you ever do that again, you hear me?"

She kissed me over and over and reached out to grab Frank and pull him to us. She kissed his face.

"Oh my babies. Don't you ever do that again."

She hugged us and kissed us and said silent prayers. She then took my face in her hands and looked into my eyes.

"Are you okay, baby?"

"I'm okay."

"I'm sorry I didn't call and let you know we were runnin' behind," Jack said as he approached home plate where we were standing. "I didn't . . ."

My mother threw her arms around him and hugged him with all her strength. She had cut him off. But this was a different kind of cut-off.

"Thank you," she said. "Thank you."

She kissed his cheek, hugging him even harder.

"Happy to do it," Jack answered.

I spotted Uncle Pat standing behind Frank.

"You got on the wrong bus on purpose."

Both Frank and I nodded our heads. Uncle Pat stepped closer and I started to pull back, fearing the worst, fearing that big, rough hand would land on my body, but he embraced both of us and held onto us to his chest as tight as he could.

"You scared the hell out of us."

And then I saw tears fall from his eyes.

"I don't know what we'd have done if we'd lost you," he said. "I just don't know."

After a moment, Uncle Pat looked toward Jack. He took a breath, let go of us, and extended his hand.

"Thank you."

Jack took Uncle Pat's hand and they shook.

"You're welcome."

I sat quietly in the backseat of the police cruiser as it pulled away from Yankee Stadium. Uncle Pat was up front with Officer Halloran and my mother was in back with her arms wrapped around Frank and me. In our hands we had brand new baseball gloves, stiff as a starched collar and each autographed by every Yankee on the roster of 1969.

"They're not gonna believe this." Frank said.

"Who's not gonna believe it?" Uncle Pat asked.

"Nobody. Nobody's gonna believe this. But we got the gloves to prove it."

Frank was beside himself, reveling in the un-questioned street cred he would soon be spreading up and down Waring Avenue. But my eyes were fixed on Gate 27. That's where Jack stood waving goodbye.

We were about to pull into traffic on One Hundred Sixtieth Street when I yelled, "STOP!"

Officer Halloran hit the brakes out of surprise as much as anything else and I immediately tried to open the back door.

"It doesn't open from the inside of the car," Officer Halloran said.

"Let me out, you gotta let me out!"

Uncle Pat turned around.

"Mickey. What do you . . ."

"Let him go," my mother said.

And Uncle Pat got out and opened the rear door. In an instant I was running toward Gate 27.

"Jack! . . . Jack!"

He turned at the sound of my voice and caught me in his arms as I leapt into his body. I held him as tight as I could and saw his eyes close as he pulled me close.

We didn't speak during the embrace. We just held it, and felt it. And let all the love it contained pour back and forth between us. It was one of the great hugs of my life. When we had taken all of it in, he placed me down, then I spoke.

"I want you to have this."

I pulled the silver dollar from my pocket.

"For luck with the number."

Jack looked at me, his eyes were flushed and his hand trembled as he reached out and took the coin.

"Would you mind if I just kept it with me all of the time?" He said with a quake in his voice. "For luck on everything?"

"Sure."

"Then that's what I'm gonna do." And he slid the coin deep into his pants pocket. "You go on now. And make us proud."

"I will."

I stood a moment longer, taking him in, pulling him into my heart and my memory, and then I turned and started for the police car.

"Hey."

I turned as Jack pulled a brand-new, shiny white baseball from the inside pocket of his old jacket.

"Glove ain't much use without one of these."

I held up my new glove, which I was surprised to discover was still on my hand. Jack squinted his eyes, then reared back like a pitcher and fired a fastball. It snapped through the air like a bolt of lightning and landed dead center in my glove, which I hadn't moved a centimeter.

"Whoa . . . You really did strike out DiMaggio."

"What you think?"

Then he smiled that wide-open smile, turned, and walked through the gate, disappearing into the stadium.

Chapter Sixteen

My mother made sure we each took a good hot bath when we got home. It was hours past our bedtime, but that didn't matter. She'd been searching for us most of the night and wasn't ready to see us off to bed. She also wanted to clean the city from our skin. She wanted the cake of soap, the drop of lavender, and the silky hot water to scrub away all the day's struggles. She wanted the scented steam to filter through our pores and circulate through our beings as if it were washing away a bad memory instead of simply dirt and grime. When we climbed from the tub, she was waiting with towels fresh out of the dryer and couldn't help but hug us once again as she wrapped them around our damp shoulders.

She also fed us. Peanut butter and jelly sandwiches spread out on cinnamon raison bread and washed down by tall glasses of ice-cold milk. And for desert we were each allowed one handful of Frito-Lay corn chips, which we chose to add directly onto our sandwiches.

Since we arrived home my mother had told us countless times how much she loved us, but that wasn't enough for her; she needed to do more, she needed to show us how much she loved us. In every way a person can show their children they love them. But I knew there was more to it than just that. She was fighting the helplessness she felt while we were gone. The same helplessness she felt since my father had gone. She wanted to erase it from her consciousness, wipe it away to the furthest reaches of her soul, and the only way she knew how was to take charge of the small details of life, to reclaim her place in our lives as protector and provider. And we were happy to have her do it.

When we finally climbed into our beds in the wee hours of the day, our minds and bodies were exhausted. Frank lay back against his pillow and slowly broke in his new glove with olive oil and string. All the while talking and talking about our run around Yankee Stadium, about how nobody was going to believe it.

I lay quietly, as was my way, and listened to my brother's musings as my mind revisited the full course of our day. Allowing myself to drift back over the entire experience. Reliving all that was done, and all that was said.

Somewhere along the way Frank fell asleep, mid-sentence, glove still in his hand. I whispered his name, but he didn't answer. I lay still, glancing at the Milky Way Frank painted on our ceiling, and then I picked up the photo from the nightstand, the one with my father. I looked at it closely, with more care than I ever had looked before. I noticed the way he squeezed each of our shoulders as he held his arms around us. I noticed the smile on his lips and the light in his eyes and I remembered it was my mom who took the picture. I could now see he was smiling not by rote, not for the simple process of taking a photograph, but for my mom. He was smiling at my mom, and he was saying to her, "Look at our boys. We did this." I could see that now, and the photo became that much more to me.

Under the amber glow of a single light, in the bathroom just outside her bedroom, my mother covered her face with cold cream and wiped it clear with a hand towel my father pilfered on their honeymoon. Her breathing was still shallow, but growing stronger. Her children were home, in their beds, and this provided comfort. But it had been a difficult day and she knew there were more such days ahead. So despite the hour, despite the tired ache she felt in her bones, she kept to her nightly rituals, the small nuances of her life that held her feet steady on decks made slippery by the tall waves of stormy seas.

She looked in the mirror and wondered where she'd gone. Where was the young woman who looked in this mirror last summer? She was no longer here. And she would never return.

It's difficult to think in terms of never and always. Their duration is too long. And when what you're thinking of is loss, when it's heartbreak, when it's blame, words such as *never* and *always* crush with the force of a toppling mountain. My mother was given much to stand, but she was also given the strength to stand it. Of this I was certain.

She struck the light and stepped into her bedroom and found me standing alone, waiting for her.

"Mickey?"

I didn't say anything. I simply stood in the darkness. The darkness would make it easier. What I had to do would be easier in the dark.

"Mickey, you're scaring me. Are you okay, baby?"

I felt the words grow inside me. Felt them start in the pit of my stomach and work their way through me until they found my throat. But it was giving them voice that would take the great leap of faith. The faith that saying them aloud wouldn't bring greater pain and retribution, but comfort.

"Mickey . . ."

I took one last breath.

"It's okay to be mad at God for what he made us stand."

"Oh baby."

"He gave us both too much. He gave us too much and it's okay we tell him that. It's okay to tell him we're mad at him."

My mother quickly crossed the room and got down on her knees in front of me.

"Jack said there's nothin' nobody can say to make us feel it wasn't our fault. Your fault and my fault."

"It wasn't your fault, baby, not at all."

"He said all we can do is say we forgive ourselves a little every day."

"Baby, baby . . ."

She wrapped her arms around me and held me tight.

"Mama . . ."

I had a little further to go, one more step, the biggest step of my life, and I called on the courage I earned that day, the courage given me by Jack.

"Mama . . ."

"Baby . . ."

The silence waited for me, challenged me—and I rose to meet it. I found my strength. I found my voice.

"I dropped my glass."

And then it poured out of me, a scream from the depths of my being, from every ounce of flesh, from every cell, it poured out of me with the force of a hurricane. The scream I couldn't scream in the coffee shop, the scream that traveled inside me for the past seven months but I wouldn't let out. It ripped through the night, through the darkness, through the silence, all the way to the heavens, to God, to my father, carrying with it all the pain and the suffering and the anguish and the torment that held me prisoner. I screamed until my body ran out of air.

"It's okay, baby. It's okay. Let it out. Just let it out."

"I dropped my glass; that's why he turned."

The tears burst from my eyes. Old tears, tears born December 17th, 1968. They'd built up behind a dam of shame and self-loathing, but the barricade had been breached. Not torn down, not toppled from its moorings, but breached. Enough of a fissure cut through to let flow the river it had held back for far too long. And I poured that river into my mother's neck, my body heaving with each sob, and with each sob a measure of relief. My hands dug into her, holding on for life and love. And love is what was given.

"It's okay baby. We love you. Daddy and I love you and it's okay."

My scream had reverberated through the house and startled Frank in his bed. And I could feel him now, standing behind me, watching me pour myself into my mother, into safety, into a place where healing might begin. And I felt his hand rest on my back, telling me it was okay, to let it go. And I did. I'm not sure for how long, maybe an hour, maybe five. But my mother and brother held me as long as I needed it, as long as it took me to empty all I had harbored.

Slowly, in time, calm and quiet returned to the room. And there was nothing but the three of us, no, the four of us, because my father was there. And in the cool darkness my mom looked into my face and through eyes wet with tears she spoke to me.

"I forgive myself today."

She kept her eyes on me, holding me with them, and through them, she gave me her love and her strength and her courage. We would do this together. We would do it as a family. And we would do it now.

I looked into my mother's eyes. Eyes filled with the power to grant wishes and make dreams come true, and I said it aloud.

"I forgive myself today."

Chapter Seventeen

Despite the relatively few hours we slept that evening, and irrespective of all the events of the prior day, come 7:00 a.m. Frank and I once again waited in front of our house for the old, coughing bus to Camp Silver Birch. My mother was uncertain about the wisdom of such action, and I could fully understand and appreciate her call for pause, but I insisted upon it, and I think Frank would have exploded without the opportunity to hold his new glove over everyone's head. My glove, however, stayed home. I had yet to decide if this was a glove to be used or cherished. More than likely one day it would be both, but that day was not yet here.

However, the bus never came. In response to a phone call placed by Mother at 6:00 a.m. sharp, the call in which she aired-out the director of our piece-of-crap camp for not having a proper mechanism in place for counting children boarding the end-of-day buses, not to mention hiring a veritable sociopath as a driver, no bus was sent to our home. Instead, Louise McCafferty came to pick up Frank and me in her brand-new, convertible MG as if we were Joe Willy Namath himself. Louise was the nineteen-year-old director of arts and crafts at Silver Birch and for the next thirty years the barometer by which I judged all women wearing short shorts and a halter top.

By noon, Frank and I were not simply the talk of the camp, we were legends. If possible, my brother had surpassed his own personal threshold of popularity and it suited him well. And I found myself for the first time in my memory as the co-center of attention. I was popular. And I experienced all the trimmings presented by such a position in the Hierarchy of Man.

The musty, moldy locker-room was especially raucous that day as an army of pre-teen city boys battled for the right to try on Frank's new glove. As a result we were slow to get ready, not quite into our cut-off shorts when the pool counselor barked from his office door.

"All right, the pool's ours. When I blow the whistle I want everybody to get a buddy so I know who drowns. And no nonsense today or I'll kick your asses."

He blew the whistle and once again the room erupted in chaos. But there was something different about this day. This day, both Frank and I were overrun with suitors. Diplomat that he is, Frank settled on two buddies, forming a trifecta of buddydom unequaled in the annals of Silver Birch.

"Mickey, let's buddy up and get out there while all those knockers are still in the pool."

I turned to my old buddy. "Not today."

Offers kept pouring in, but I brushed aside all my new-found admirers and walked to the far reaches of the locker room.

"Buddy up?"

Nelson was seated on the back bench, still in his play clothes. He hadn't bothered to change into his cut-offs. When I said those words his head was down, looking at his feet which swung back and forth beneath him. But now he looked up.

"Mickey . . ."

I didn't have to turn around to see who it was. It didn't matter. It was one voice but it might as well have been all of them. Without looking I could see them all shrinking away from me, pulling back, disavowing me, Louise McCafferty and Yankee Stadium or not.

I looked at Nelson.

"Well?"

"Buddy up," he said.

"Then let's get movin'."

A smile broke across Nelson's face as he quickly tore off his play clothes and pulled on his cut-offs. In my mind I was thinking of what Jack said to me. That a man is not what he says, but what he does. And that my childhood was gone, stolen from me that day in December, so I had to be a man, as soon as possible, that would be the only way I would survive.

"All right, grab your buddy," shouted the pool counselor.

He blew his whistle and I held out my hand to Nelson. Nelson smiled at me and took it.

Jack was right. I was only seven years old, but I had to start becoming the man I would be. I decided this day would be that day.

Coda

By the end of summer we had said our goodbyes to the Bronx and moved to New Jersey with my Uncle Pat. It was strange at first and the adjustment took time, but Jack was right about him. Given half the chance, Uncle Pat was quite a man. He was all about taking care of his brother's children and as a surrogate father showed more love and tenderness then I thought he possessed. My mother said having us boys around softened Uncle Pat, and I can honestly say he was one of the finest men I've ever known. I miss him dearly.

Though we moved from New York, Frank and I still saw Jack from time to time, but never as much as I would have liked. Whenever Uncle Pat took us to a Yankee game we'd be sure to arrive early and stay late so we could spend some time with him. A few times Jack brought us into the dugout during batting practice to meet some of the ballplayers and he'd always sneak us some wonderful piece of memorabilia along with a warning not to be stealin' like he's stealin'.

But as the years past we saw less and less of him. The last time our paths crossed was my rookie season,

1990. My gift of catching round objects proved more valuable then I first suspected. I had come up through the Kansas City farm system and was called up to play with the big team on July 18th. My first series on the road was at Yankee Stadium.

I hadn't seen or spoken to Jack in over six years. I didn't know what to expect. In many ways I was more nervous about seeing him than playing my first major league ballgame in the *House That Ruth Built*. But as I walked into the visitors' clubhouse with my team, I saw that smile, with all the love and excitement I hoped it would have. We embraced tightly before a word was exchanged, and I knew he felt as I felt, that in some ways his son had finally made the big leagues.

"You forgive yourself a little bit today?" I heard him whisper before looking at me with his heart wide open.

"There's nothing to forgive," I replied.

"Good. That's good."

We spent the next four days together. Jack and Frank and me. We laughed, cried, and remembered that day, each of us in our own way. It was a wonderful weekend. And it reminded me that Jack is always with me. Like my father is. People who give of themselves are like that. They stay with you. And that's what I hope to be one day as well.

In the summer of 1999, on a hot, muggy day that melted into a hotter, muggier night, I sat in the passenger seat of Frank's new BMW 5-Series as we crossed the

George Washington Bridge from North Jersey. In back were our two sons. His boy Billy had just turned nine, and my son Jack was two months shy of eight.

"Dad, after your dead, doesn't a guy pull your guts out?" asked Frank's son.

"Well, I don't know that he pulls, but removal is the basic idea," Frank answered.

"Why do they pull your guts out?" My son wanted to know.

"So you don't rot and start stinkin' before they can put you in the ground."

"Frank, give me a break."

Frank glanced at me, smiled his devilish smile, and started working the radio in search of the perfect song.

"How come we gotta go see a dead guy we don't know?" came a voice from the back.

"Cause we know him," I said.

"So why do we have to go?"

"Because there are people you should meet."

Frank followed the signs to Harlem.

Several years after Jack retired from the New York Yankees his body began to give out. His sister Grace offered to put him up but Jack chose to return south, to Shreveport, where he lived with his nephew until he died. We spoke by phone on occasion but his difficulty with breathing kept our conversations short. Generally just long enough for Jack to tell me my swing was for crap. That he'd have *struck me out on three pitches if he was blindfolded and throwing with his foot*.

When we parked in front of Belkins Funeral Home on One Hundred Fortieth Street I could see our sons were nervous. When we stepped from the car my son Jack slipped his hand into mine.

"You knew this guy?"

Frank looked at me and smiled. "Yeah, we knew him."

We entered the building and quietly made our way toward a door where two young black boys about six were standing beside a large poster-sized photo of Jack in his uniform from the Bacharach Giants.

"Remember that photo?" Frank smiled.

"Sure do."

I held out my hand to the two boys standing by the photo.

"I'm sorry about your uncle."

"He wasn't our uncle. He was our great-uncle."

"No, he was our great, great uncle," the second one corrected.

"Yes he was. I'm Mike, this is my brother Frank, and these are our sons Jack and Billy."

"Jack was my uncle's name."

"Great, great uncle," the second boy reminded.

"He was named after your great, great uncle," I said.

The four youngsters looked at each other the way youngsters who don't know each other look at one another. Then the door to the viewing room suddenly flew open and a woman about thirty-five stood in the doorway.

"What's twelve times thirteen?"

Frank smiled. "Don't you start with me."

"You're just mad cause you don't know."

"Jack, Billy," I said to our boys, "I'd like you to meet Judge Rose Phillips."

"Hi."

Rose hugged Frank, then hugged me.

"I'm so glad you're here."

She held us a moment more, then let go and turned toward my son.

"So you're Jack?"

"Yes," he said.

"My uncle left something for me to give to you."

She then reached into her jacket pocket and retrieved a silver dollar minted in the year 1962.

"I don't believe it," Frank said.

Rose handed the coin to my son.

"He said this will bring you luck. Always. Just like it did for him."

"Thank you," my son replied.

I kissed Rose on the cheek and whispered.

"Thank you."

She smiled, "Let's go in and say goodbye."

On the way home we drove quietly, no talking and no music. But as we pulled into the house I shared with my son Jack, my wife Linda and my two-month-old daughter, Grace, Frank asked me what I remembered most about that day all those years ago. He was surprised by my answer. It wasn't how Jack helped me through a painful time, or how we nearly got run down by a subway car, or how we ran around Yankee Stadium, having that glorious building all to ourselves. But rather it was something Jack said as he sat in Dizzy's Diner eating his baby-backs:

"Two ears, two eyes, same as you."

About The Author

After graduating with distinction from Gettysburg College and the American University Washington College of Law, Robert Pucci passed the bar exams for both New York and New Jersey, then promptly moved to Los Angeles to become an actor. (On quiet nights you can still hear his mother screaming.) While playing a recurring role on "The Young & The Restless," he realized that at heart, he is a writer.

Robert has sold over twenty-five screenplays to such studios as Paramount, Sony, Warner Brothers, Fox, Universal and Miramax, and has worked with, among others, Oliver Stone, Jan Debont, James Foley, Mark Wahlberg, Roland Joffee and Diane Keaton.

People Magazine said that his script for the television movie "The Spider & The Fly, " "...contains more twists and turns than an old, knotted phone cord."

The New York Times wrote regarding his script for the feature film "The Corruptor," "Robert Pucci has managed to turn a meat-and-potatoes action flick into a cunning meditation on personal loyalty and situational morality."

With "In Harlem's Way," his first novel, Robert continues telling stories and creating characters that examine the complexities of the human heart.

www.robertpucci.com

3936371R00133

Made in the USA
San Bernardino, CA
25 August 2013